GRANDMA'S
ATTIC NOVELS

A School of Her Own

ARLETA RICHARDSON

Cook Communications

**You'll enjoy all the books in
Arleta Richardson's
Grandma's Attic Collection**

In Grandma's Attic

More Stories from Grandma's Attic

Still More Stories from Grandma's Attic

Treasures from Grandma

Away from Home

A School of Her Own

Wedding Bells Ahead

At Home in North Branch

New Faces, New Friends

"LOOK OUT BEHIND YOU! HE'S GOING TO KNOCK YOU DOWN!"

I looked around to see a huge billy goat, head down, charging in my direction. There was no time to consider a ladylike reaction. I hoisted my skirt in both hands and galloped for the barn as fast as I could go. As I reached the door, a tall young man came running out. Without a second thought, I grabbed him around the neck. He lifted me off the ground and out of the way as the goat barreled through the door and into the barn.

"Why in the world don't you have that animal tethered?" I sputtered. "He could have butted me into the next county!" Suddenly I realized that the young man was still holding me. "And please put me down."

Mabel's career as a schoolteacher wasn't off to a very dignified start. . . .

Cook Communications Ministries,
Colorado Springs, Colorado 80918
Cook Communications, Paris, Ontario
Kingsway Communications, Eastbourne, England

A SCHOOL OF HER OWN
© 1986 by Arleta Richardson

Previously titled EIGHTEEN AND ON HER OWN

Cover illustration by Steve Armes, PGS Advertising
Cover design by Manoutch Kazemzadeh, PGS Advertising

First printing, 1986
Printed in the United States of America
04 03 02 01 00   5 4 3 2 1

Library of Congress Cataloging-in-Publication Data

Richardson, Arleta
        Eighteen and a school of her own.
        Summary: Fresh out of school herself, eighteen-year-old
Mabel takes a teaching job in a farming community similar to the
one where she grew up.
[1. Teachers—Fiction. 2. Schools—Fiction. 3. Farm life—Fiction]
1. Title
PZ7.R3942Ei   1986   [Fic]   85-29050
ISBN: 0-78143-291-X

For Uncle Clare and Aunt Billie
whom I love very much

Contents

Eighteen

"MA, DO I LOOK ALL RIGHT?" I WHIRLED around to let her inspect my new outfit. The pale blue skirt was fashionably long, and the white batiste blouse had tiny tucks and pleats down the front. "Everyone will know *I* didn't make this," I said with a laugh. "My patience would have given out on the first tuck."

Impulsively I hugged Ma. "I can't believe I'm actually ready to teach school."

I turned to look in the mirror over the sink and patted the curls that had been swept smoothly to the top of my head and held in place with tortoise-shell combs. The grey green eyes that looked back at me were shining with excitement. This was my last summer before I would have to settle down and be grown up.

"You'd better get out there," Ma suggested. "Your guests will be arriving any minute. On your way, tell Pa to come and get ready. No doubt he's lost track of the time."

I detoured to the barn in search of Pa, who

was carrying the last of the feed to the cows. "Ma says you're to hurry," I told him.

He turned around and surveyed me fondly. "Eighteen," he said. "There were times when I didn't think we'd get you past your childhood. You've been a good daughter, Mabel."

I reached out and hugged him.

"Be careful," he objected. "You'll get that pretty dress dirty."

"I don't care, Pa. It's more important to hug you. You've been a good father, too. I don't know what I've done to deserve a family like mine."

"Now don't get teary eyed, or you'll ruin your dress. Run along now, and I'll go get ready. I imagine your ma has all the Sunday duds laid out."

Friends and neighbors began to gather on the big front lawn that had been the scene of so many happy occasions. The Clarks had arrived; I saw Mrs. Clark go into the kitchen to help Ma. I went to look for Sarah Jane.

"Look who's coming," she said, giggling. "And he's actually carrying a basket of food that still has the cover on it." She pointed to Wesley Patterson, who had come with his parents.

"He had an escort," I said. "Wesley wouldn't dare open that food basket with his mother looking on."

10

Wesley delivered the food to the kitchen, and then came toward us.

"He hasn't gotten any smaller around," Sarah Jane noted, "but he is taller."

"Mabel. Sarah Jane." Wesley held out his hand awkwardly, and we shook hands with him. "Did you have a good year at school?"

I started to answer when Sarah Jane turned away and leaned up against a tree, her shoulders shaking.

Wesley looked perplexed. "Did I say something wrong? Is she crying?"

"I don't think so," I replied. "Sarah Jane, for goodness' sake—" Then I couldn't help it; I began to laugh. Wesley stood by, smiling uncertainly.

"I'm sorry," Sarah Jane gasped. "Forgive me, Wesley. I just couldn't help remembering how we tried to make you lose weight by taking your lunch. I'm ashamed when I think how mean we were to you, but it was funny." She laughed again, and this time Wesley joined her.

"I don't blame you," he said when we had calmed down. "Pa says I still eat twice as much as the rest of the family put together, but he wouldn't know what to do without me. And I do twice as much work, too! We've bought an extra fifty acres that will be mine when I am married."

"Married!" I exclaimed. "We didn't hear about that."

"Oh, not yet!" Wesley answered. "I don't have any plans right now." He blushed and looked across the yard. "I am keeping company with Hannah, though. She's a great cook. Well, I'll see you later." He moved off toward Hannah, and Sarah Jane shook her head.

"Wesley has not misjudged his calling," she said. "A farm is the only thing that could ever support him."

"Oh, there's Mrs. Porter!" Our beloved teacher, who had been Miss Gibson for eight years of our school life, was coming through the gate. We ran to meet her.

"Mabel! Sarah Jane!" She tried to hug both of us at the same time. "I'm so proud of the two of you for graduating with honors! I knew you could do it. And, Mabel—" she held me off and smiled at me. "You still managed to equal Warren Carter in everything except math. Did he outdo you with the same two points?"

I nodded. "And he deserved it. I was happy that he won the scholarship to college. I've applied for a school, and I can finish my education in the summers."

"You'll make an excellent teacher, Mabel. I'm sure you've learned a lot of new things to try in your own school."

"We'll sit down and talk later," I told her. "We have so much to tell you. I wish you could meet Molly and Thomas and Russ."

"Did I hear someone mention my name?" said a voice.

I whirled around to face a grinning Molly Matson.

"Molly! Where . . .? How . . .? Sarah Jane, did you know she was coming? And you didn't tell me?"

"Of course," Sarah Jane answered. "I don't tell you everything I know. Warren and I decided that the rest of the troops shouldn't miss out on something as important as this. Where are the fellows, Molly?"

"They were right behind me," Molly replied. "They'll be here any minute."

I looked toward the gate. I was sure Thomas Charles would have come to see Sarah Jane, but had Russ really come, too? Russ Bradley—tall and handsome and my special friend during the two years of high school.

I didn't wonder long. Warren appeared with Thomas and Russ, and Sarah Jane ran to meet them.

"Are you coming?" Molly asked me. "Russ is awfully anxious to see you."

When I held back, Molly laughed. "Come on. Don't pretend you didn't know how he

13

feels about you. Are you getting shy all of a sudden?"

She grabbed my hand and pulled me toward the others, and we were soon chattering as though we'd been apart three years instead of just three weeks.

"The town is awfully quiet with all of you gone," Russ said.

"We'll have to plan to get together more this summer before everyone goes in different directions."

"Russ and I are going to room together at the university," Warren said. "And Thomas will be there, too. Have you girls gotten your schools yet?"

I shook my head. "No, but we've just applied. I'm sure we'll hear before too long. It frightens me to think about going for an interview."

"You?" Molly exclaimed. "You always know what to say!"

"And if she doesn't, she makes it up," Sarah Jane put in. "I've known Mabel since before we could walk, and she's never been speechless. And most of the time she even makes sense!" She grinned at me good-naturedly.

"What I say will be important this time," I insisted. "Everything depends upon it—— my career . . . my whole life!"

"Well, maybe not your *whole* life," Molly said. "You'll probably get married before too long."

"Definitely not," I replied. "Marriage is not on my agenda. I've worked hard to be able to teach, and I plan to teach!"

"I've worked hard, too," Sarah Jane chimed in, "but I'll consider other options." Then she turned red as Warren poked Thomas and snickered.

"How is Clarice?" I said quickly.

"You're the last one I'd expect to hear asking about Clarice Owens," said Molly. "You haven't forgotten all the hard times she gave you, have you?"

"Never. She was a pain, but I learned some things from her, too. Besides, you'll have to admit that she was nicer the second year."

"I prefer my learning in easier doses," said Sarah Jane. "Clarice just finally realized the futility of hating someone who refuses to hate you back. What's she doing this summer, anyway?"

"She's gone with her folks to visit relatives in the east," Russ replied. "Lettie and Jacob were certainly relieved that Mrs. Owens took Clarice along instead of asking them to look after her again!"

At the mention of Lettie and Jacob, I felt a twinge of homesickness for the little room we

15

had occupied during high school days and the loving couple who had looked after us so well.

"We'll have to come visit for a few days before school starts," Sarah Jane said.

"Good idea!" Thomas exclaimed. "Warren can come at the same time, and we'll have great fun."

"Mercy!" I said. "I've been sitting here all this time and ignoring my other guests! Come on—let me introduce you to the neighbors you haven't met."

Mrs. Gibbs beamed at Russ as she pumped his hand. "So this is Mabel's young man. You're getting a fine young lady here," she told him. "I've known Mabel all her life, and if I had a son eligible to marry her, you wouldn't have a chance, I'll tell you!"

I was ready to hide behind a tree with embarrassment, but Russ seemed not in the least disturbed. He smiled and replied, "I know that, ma'am. And thank you."

"Maybe I'd better see if Ma needs any help," I said quickly. "It must be almost time to eat."

"This is your birthday, Mabel," Sarah Jane reminded me. "There are lots of people who can help. You just stay here with your young man, and Molly and I will go check to see if everything is under control."

With wicked little grins, they ran off across the lawn.

"Don't pay attention to their teasing," Russ laughed. "I can think of worse things to be called than your young man. I wanted to ask if I could write to you this winter, Mabel. I know we'll both be pretty busy, but I don't want to lose you."

Later that evening, I told Molly and Sarah Jane what Russ had said. "He sounded awfully serious. I don't think I'm ready for this."

"For goodness' sake, Mabel," said Sarah Jane. "You know Russ can't begin to think about getting married until he finishes college. That's four more years! By that time you may have had all the teaching you want. I'm sure *I* will," she added with a sigh.

"You'll never find anyone nicer than Russ, Mabel," Molly put in. "And the fact that he's going into the bank with his father when he graduates is certainly no drawback. Most young men his age don't know what they'll be doing four years from now."

"Now hold on a minute!" I protested. "You two engineered the first evening Russ and I spent together, but I'm not going to let you arrange my whole life! I know what a nice fellow he is, and I like him a lot, but I'm just not prepared to make that kind of decision.

When I am, you'll be the first to know."

"All right, Mabel," Sarah Jane said. "One would think that after all these years you'd realize that I have your best interests at heart. Don't blame me if you reach your thirtieth birthday and find that Russ has married someone else and you're destined to live a lonely life, going to school day after day, year after year—"

"You should be on the stage," I interrupted. "You'll have us sobbing in a minute. But I'll tell you what I realize. Practically everything that has gotten me into trouble since I learned to walk has been the result of your 'best interests.'"

"What more could you ask of a friend?" Molly said with a shrug. "At least the two of you were in it together."

———2———
Is This
God's Will?

IS THERE ANY MAIL FOR ME, PA?" I HAD hurried out to the barn when I saw him coming from town.

"Were you looking for mail?" he teased.

"You know I am. Did I hear from North Branch yet?"

"No, I'm afraid not," Pa replied, "but will this do instead?" He handed me a letter from Russ Bradley, which I slipped into my pocket to read later.

"Thanks, Pa. I'm glad to hear from Russ, but I really want to hear about school. I was so sure I had a chance when I went for the interview. What do you think is holding them up?"

Pa lifted the parcels out of the buggy and we started toward the house. "It hasn't been a month yet," he said. "It takes time for a school board to get together and consider all the applicants."

"All the applicants! Pa, you know there were only two of us, and the other was a man. He can apply someplace else. He told me he didn't care where he went because he's only going to teach for one year. I'm planning to make it my life's work."

Pa looked at me quizzically. "That's pretty ambitious planning. Are you sure that's what the Lord wants you to do with the rest of your life?"

"I never thought about it not being," I replied. "He made the way for me to finish school and get a teacher's certificate. Isn't that proof enough of his will? He could have stopped me at any time."

Pa looked thoughtful, but he didn't say any more about it. Later, as we did dishes, I brought the subject up with Ma.

"Ma, what did you plan to do with your life?"

She stopped with a dish half washed and stared at me in surprise.

"I mean when you were my age."

"Reuben was a year old when I was your age," she laughed. "I didn't have many plans beyond surviving in the windy log cabin we lived in. Why do you ask?"

"Did the Lord tell you to marry Pa?"

"No, I don't recall that he did."

"Then how do you know it was the Lord's will?" I persisted. "What if you married the wrong man? You weren't very old."

"That's right," Ma agreed. "I was fifteen

20

years old when we were married on Christmas Day. I didn't turn sixteen till January. Why do you ask? Do you think I married the wrong man?"

"Oh, Ma! Of course I don't! I wouldn't want anyone but Pa. But how did you *know*?"

"I really never thought about that, Mabel," Ma replied. "I do believe that the steps of a good man are ordered by the Lord. And in Jeremiah the Bible tells us that the Lord knows the plans he has for us; plans for good and not for evil. That sounds pretty certain, doesn't it?"

After supper, Sarah Jane came over and we wandered down to the brook to see how the blueberries were coming.

"You know," I told her, "it sounds to me as though we're wasting our time trying to decide what we want to do when we grow up. It looks like God already has it worked out and all we can do is go along with it."

"I don't think so, Mabel," she disagreed. "If it worked that way, we'd never make any wrong choices or decisions—and goodness knows we've made plenty of those in our lifetime! Do you think God had it all worked out for you to throw your history notes in the fire and carry your scrap paper to school?"

I laughed. "No, that was my fault. It was just carelessness. But maybe God allowed it to show me that I needed to pay more attention to what I was doing."

"What made you think about all this, anyway?" Sarah Jane wanted to know.

"Pa asked me if I was sure it would be God's will for me to teach for the rest of my life."

"So you think if it is, there's nothing you can do about it. You'll have to teach whether you want to or not."

"I'm not sure what I think," I replied. "I'm just trying to decide how much is up to me and how much is up to God."

"I'd say it's up to you to get an education and apply for a school, and up to God to see that you get it if he wants you to have it. You didn't hear from North Branch today, huh?"

"No, but I just remembered—I *did* get a letter from Russ." I pulled it out of my pocket.

"You mean you haven't even *opened* it yet? Oh, Mabel, you are impossible!"

"I forgot all about it," I admitted. "But I'm sure it isn't old news yet; it just came this morning." I tore open the envelope and read the letter out loud.

Dear Mabel,

How is your summer going? I've been working with my father in the bank to earn extra money for school. As you know, Warren Carter and I will be rooming together at the university this fall. We are looking forward to it. Too bad we won't have your competition to keep us on our toes!

I am writing to invite you to spend the day in town on the 25th of July. Thomas is asking Sarah Jane to come also. The county fair will be open, and we could have a great day together. Drop me a card to say you're coming, and we'll meet you a week from Saturday.

Yours truly,
Russ

"Thomas didn't write to me!" Sarah Jane said. "At least I didn't get a letter this morning. Do you think we should go?"

"I don't know why not," I replied. "It sounds like fun. We can go on the early train and come back in the evening. I'll write and tell him we'll be there."

Ma was pleased about the invitation. "That's a nice idea, Mabel. You've worked hard this summer, and school will be starting before you know it."

"Besides," Pa added with a twinkle, "Ma likes that young man. If he were a few years older, he'd make a good son-in-law."

"He couldn't be your son-in-law unless he married me," I retorted, "and I'm not getting married. It's not in my plans. At least it's not unless the Lord wills otherwise," I added.

"Maybe that's the answer to your question," Ma said. "Make all your preparations subject to God's pleasure, and you'll never be disappointed."

Sarah Jane's letter came, and we sent a card accepting their invitation. A week seemed a long time to wait.

"Now to decide what to wear," Sarah Jane said. "What do you think?"

"Anything that's cool," I declared. "How about your flowered muslin?"

"Mmm, I guess so. And you could wear your dotted swiss. For goodness' sake, Mabel, don't get any ideas about making something new for the occasion! I couldn't stand to miss the train while you were putting in the last stitches."

"How many times have you missed a train because of me?" I asked. "Honestly, Sarah Jane, you don't give me credit for the sense God gave a goose!"

"Maybe that much," she allowed. "But you know from past experience how often you need a keeper."

"And you know from past experience that you'd better not apply for the job. But this trip is going off without a hitch. You'll see."

Saturday dawned without a cloud in sight.

Pa offered to take us to the train, and we stopped for Sarah Jane in front of her gate.

"Now you girls have a good time today," Pa instructed, as he let us out at the depot. "I'll be here to pick you up when the train comes in this evening."

"Thanks, Pa. We'll see you later."

The telegraph machine was clacking when we entered the station, but no one was around.

"Where's the station master?" Sarah Jane wondered. "It's almost time for the train to be in."

"Where is *everybody*?" I said. "There are always more passengers than this. Or at least people waiting for someone to come in."

We went over and looked through the ticket window. "Mr. Barnes," I called. "May we get a ticket?"

Mr. Barnes appeared from a back room. "How's that?"

"A ticket," I repeated. "We want to go to Rosemond."

"Train's gone. Left an hour ago."

"An hour ago! But it's not seven-thirty yet!" Sarah Jane protested.

"That's true," Mr. Barnes agreed. "But that's not got much to do with it." He pointed with his thumb to a sign on the wall and returned to the back room.

SCHEDULE CHANGE FOR
GRAND TRUNK RAILWAY
EFFECTIVE JULY 15, 1891

"This is the trip that was going without a hitch," Sarah Jane moaned. "If I were ten years younger, I'd bawl."

"I may bawl anyway," I said. "Do you realize that Pa has gone, and we have no way to get back home except to walk?"

We sank down on a bench to consider the possibilities.

"This is *not* what I had in mind when I got out of bed this morning," Sarah Jane declared. "What do we do now?"

"Do you suppose Mr. Barnes would send a telegram to tell the boys we missed the train?" I said. "We'll have to let them know somehow. I hate for them to find out that we didn't have the brains to check the train schedule."

"How would we know it would change all of a sudden?" Sarah Jane asked crossly. "It's never changed before."

"Yep, I could do that," Mr. Barnes assured us when we asked. "What's the name? Wait just a minute. There's a message coming in."

When he came back to the window, he was shaking his head. "You young ladies can be glad you missed that one," he said. "The train derailed up toward Scottville. Several people injured. Somebody was looking out for you."

Sarah Jane turned pale, and we both sat down again. "We know who the 'somebody' was, Mr. Barnes," she said. "God took care of us by using our own mistake. I'm never again going to doubt that my life is planned by him."

Mr. Barnes sent our message, and we headed for home. "This is probably no farther than we would have walked at the fair," I said. "And we learned something about God's will. We can make our plans, but if we're trusting him, he'll work them out for our good."

We walked along silently for a way, thinking how good God was to protect us from danger.

"Do you suppose other people on that train were trusting God with their plans, too?" Sarah Jane asked suddenly. "Why did God protect us and not them?"

"I don't know," I admitted. "Maybe he wanted to show them that *whatever* circumstances they were in, he could take care of them. Whenever I say 'Why did God allow that?', Pa tells me that if I'm going to trust God with my life, I have to let him be God, and not question his decisions."

"I guess that's right," Sarah Jane said. "If we had all the answers, we'd be taking over his job . . . and I'm not ready for that. So," she continued, "what shall we do with the rest of our day? What have you always wanted to do and never had time for?"

"Nothing I can do in these clothes. I think by the time I get home I'm going to want to take a lunch and sit under our tree and let the world go by."

"That sounds good," Sarah Jane agreed. "There's no way we could botch up a plan like that. Is there?"

3

Mabel Gets
A School

THE LETTER FROM NORTH BRANCH finally came.

"Have you read your contract through?" Pa asked when he came in to dinner.

"Yes," I answered, "several times. Pa, I didn't know I'd have to sign my life away to be a schoolteacher."

"I've never seen a contract that demanded that," Pa said. "What part of your life are they asking for?"

"It looks to me like all of it. It's a good thing it doesn't say I can't come home weekends, or I might reconsider."

"I think the district needs to be sure that they have a teacher of high moral character to be a good example for their children," Ma said. "It sounds like a good idea to me."

"Why don't you read it to me, Mabel?" Pa suggested.

I sat down at the table and opened the contract in front of me.

School Contract—North Branch District

I promise to take a vital interest in all phases of schoolwork, donating my time, service, and money without stint for the uplifting and benefit of the community.

I promise to abstain from dancing, immodest dressing, and any other conduct unbecoming a teacher and a lady.

I promise not to go out with any young man except insofar as it may be necessary to stimulate Sunday school work.

I promise not to fall in love, become engaged, or be secretly married.

I promise to remain in my home when not actively engaged in school or church work elsewhere.

I promise not to encourage or tolerate the least familiarity on the part of any of my boy pupils.

I promise to sleep at least eight hours a night, eat carefully, and take every precaution to keep in the best of health and spirits in order that I may be better able to render efficient service to my pupils.

30

I agree to payment of $25.00 per month, beginning September 7, 1891 and ending June 17, 1892.

Signed:

*Date:*_____ *18* _____   _____
                                              Teacher

_____
President of the Board

"That sounds pretty reasonable to me," Pa said when I had finished. "Is there something in there you don't want to do?"

"Not really. It just seems odd to have to ask a school board for permission to get married."

"Since marriage isn't in your plans anyway, it shouldn't be too hard to agree to that," Pa teased.

Sarah Jane had plenty to say when we discussed it later. "I don't know why they worry about us being secretly married when we've already promised not to go out with a young man unless we're benefiting the Sunday school. I never realized what a restricted life a teacher has to lead."

"I have a feeling that by the time I study, prepare lessons, and correct papers, I'm not going to feel like leaving my room," I said.

"Do you know where you'll be boarding?"

"No, but I hope it will be one place for the whole year. Some schools have the teacher take turns at all the pupils' homes." She shuddered. "Can you imagine some of the places you might get into?"

"It doesn't look as though I'll have to worry about that," I said. "Mr. Williams told me I'd be boarding with them."

"Do they have any children in school?"

"No. There are two daughters who are already married and a son. He lives at home, but he's out of school."

"I'm anxious to know how many children I'll have, and how many grades." Sarah Jane. looked out across the field. "Does it scare you when you think that you might not be more than two years older than some of your students?"

"I've thought about it," I admitted. "Some of the boys are sure to be bigger than I am. But I keep thinking that Mrs. Porter managed her school. If she could do it, I can, too."

"We should take a day and go look at our schools," Sarah Jane suggested. "Then we'd have some idea about what we were getting into."

We decided on the following Thursday for the trip and went in to ask Pa if we could use the buggy.

The day was warm and clear when we started out early in the morning.

"Your school is first," Sarah Jane said. "We'll have to stop and get the key from the board president."

"I know where his house is," I said. "That's where I'll be living."

We arrived in less than an hour, and I knocked on the kitchen door. There was no answer, nor did I see anyone around the yard.

"It looks as though you'll have to go out to the barn, Mabel," Sarah Jane said. "Someone has to be at home on a weekday."

I turned down the path toward the barn, walking carefully so as not to catch my skirt. Suddenly I heard Sarah Jane scream.

"Mabel! Look out behind you! He's going to knock you down!"

I looked around to see a huge billy goat, head down, charging in my direction. There was no time to consider a ladylike reaction. I hoisted my skirt in both hands and galloped for the barn as fast as I could go. As I reached the door, a tall young man came running out. Without a second thought I grabbed him around the neck. He lifted me off the ground and out of the way as the goat barreled through the door and into the barn.

"Why in the world don't you have that

animal tethered?" I sputtered. "He could have butted me into the next county!" Suddenly I realized that the young man was still holding me. "And please put me down."

He set me on the ground, and closed the bottom sections of the barn door. I attempted to straighten my dress and retrieve what small amount of dignity I had left. The appearance of a breathless Sarah Jane did nothing to help, since she was laughing so hard that she had to lean against the building.

"Oh, Mabel! I haven't seen you run that fast since we were ten years old! You'll never know how you looked flying down the path with the goat three steps behind you!"

The young man, too, was having great difficulty keeping a straight face. I was not amused.

"I came to ask Mr. Williams if I might have the key to the schoolhouse," I said stiffly. "Do you know where the family is?"

"Yes, ma'am, they've gone to town. But I can get the key for you." He loped up the path to the house, and we followed at a slower pace.

"You didn't ask what his name was," Sarah Jane said. "He's awfully nice looking."

"I'm not interested," I snapped. "He's probably the hired man. And not a very good one,

I might add, if he can't keep the livestock from terrorizing the neighborhood."

"He certainly plucked you out of the way with no difficulty," Sarah Jane said. "But it was your own fault. You shouldn't have thrown yourself at him. It wasn't very proper."

"Sarah Jane, I was in no position to be proper," I retorted. "I could feel that animal *breathing* on me. Did you want to see me trampled to death?"

"No," she choked. "What I saw was enough entertainment for the rest of the summer."

"Here you are, ma'am." The young man handed me the key and helped us into the buggy. "You may leave it here on the porch when you've finished," he said.

"Thank you," I replied in the coolest voice I could manage. As we drove away, I could see the laughter in his brown eyes, although his face remained appropriately solemn.

"Insufferable person," I muttered. "I'll make sure I don't run into him again when I come back to stay."

"At least not as hard as you did this time."

"Oh, you know what I mean," I replied. "If you don't settle down, you're going to be walking home. You wouldn't think it was so funny if it had happened to you. But then, when does anything ever happen to you?"

The school wasn't far from the house. Surrounded on two sides by woods, it sat back far enough from the road so that there was a good-sized playground. The building looked the same as all the other schools in the county—white clapboard with a bell on top and a porch across the front.

"With my eyes shut, I can tell what time of year it is when I step into a schoolhouse," Sarah Jane said as we opened the door. "In the fall it smells hot and dusty. In the winter it has the odor of a wood fire and wet mittens. In the spring, when the windows are all open, it smells like new grass and leaves and perfumy flowers."

"I didn't know you had that much poetry in your soul, Sarah Jane," I said. "But you're right. This smells like a fall school."

We walked around, looking at the familiar furnishings. A stove in the corner, the teacher's desk on a small platform, four rows of desks. There was room for twenty-eight students, and for a moment I could almost see them sitting there. The windows were grimy, with big flies caught in the spiderwebs that decorated the corners.

"I wonder if the teacher is responsible for cleaning the place before school starts," I said. "Did your board say anything about cleaning the school?"

Sarah Jane shook her head. "I think they have a custodian. We can't carry wood and take out ashes and build fires. I expect someone will have the place shining before the term starts."

I sat down in the chair behind the teacher's desk. "School certainly looks different from this side of the desk. Do you think we're really ready for this?"

"You said the same thing about going away to high school, Mabel. Life keeps moving on, whether you're ready or not. We're going to get along just fine."

"I wonder where they stored the books for the summer?" I said. "Probably at the Williams home! I don't think I'll stop to inquire." I turned at the sound of Sarah Jane's snort. "Now don't you start again," I warned. "I don't know what you're going to do for amusement this winter without me."

There was no one in sight when I left the key on the back porch, and for that I was grateful.

The day grew warmer as we drove, and the road was dusty.

"There's a little stream," Sarah Jane pointed out. "Let's stop and eat lunch in the shade." Later, as we lay on the grass and looked up through the trees, this seemed to be the best of all places and times to be alive.

4

A New Chapter Begins

IT WAS LATE SUNDAY AFTERNOON WHEN PA and I arrived in North Branch. We had taken Sarah Jane to Edanville and met the lady with whom she would be living.

"Sarah Jane is glad that she can stay in one place," I told Pa, "even though Mrs. Phelps is the only person there. That might be a real advantage, not having any children in the house."

"Did you say that the Williams family had no one in school?"

I nodded. "All their children are grown. I probably should feel nervous, staying with the school board president, but Mr. Williams was so nice. I don't think I'll mind at all."

"You've lived with a school board president most of your life," Pa laughed. "We're just ordinary people who are interested in education."

I didn't tell Pa about the hired man I had met. I supposed I would see him at mealtimes, but I certainly didn't want to have any conversation with him.

Mr. Williams was standing in the doorway when we pulled up to the porch.

"Good, good," he said. "You're just in time for supper." He helped me down from the buggy, and then assisted Pa with my trunk. "We'll leave this right here. Len will carry it upstairs after we've eaten. Come in, and be at home."

We entered a large, cheerful kitchen, and Mrs. Williams bustled over to greet us. "Miss O'Dell, we're so happy to have you with us. And Mr. O'Dell, have a seat, please. We'll be ready to eat in just a few minutes. Alice," she called, "come help me put supper on, please."

A slender girl with dark hair and eyes came in from an adjoining room. "This is the new teacher, Alice. Alice is our niece," she told me. "She's living here with us until she gets married in the spring. You two are about the same age and will be good company for each other."

"Let me help you, Alice," I said. "I don't want to sit here looking like a visitor." She smiled her welcome, and together we finished setting the table.

"Call Leonard to supper, please," Mrs. Williams instructed. "And come and sit down, all of you."

I heard only one person coming down the stairs, and wondered if the hired man was gone on weekends. Then Mr. Williams was saying, "Mr. O'Dell, Miss O'Dell, I want you to meet my son, Leonard."

I turned to look once again into that pair of laughing eyes. I grabbed the back of my chair to steady myself as he shook hands with Pa. Then he held out his hand to me.

"Miss O'Dell, I'm pleased to meet you." There was nothing on his face to indicate that he had ever seen me before, let alone had me hanging around his neck! If it had not been for the mischief dancing in his eyes, I might have been able to convince myself that he had forgotten about it.

I kept my eyes on my plate as the conversation flowed around me. "I have a son about your age," Pa was saying, "and another two years older. Both my boys are married and have their own farms."

"Len hasn't found any young lady who wants to be a minister's wife," Alice offered.

"That is their loss," Pa replied. "There's no higher calling than the ministry."

"And no lower wages," Len said with a laugh. "I wouldn't ask anyone to share what I make on a country circuit. I'm glad to stay home and help Pa around here until I have a bigger church."

I felt my face grow warm. A minister! It would have been bad enough to throw myself at the hired man, but at a preacher! It was suddenly quiet, and I looked up to see all eyes on me.

"I beg your pardon," I stammered. "Did you ask me something?"

"Yes," Mr. Williams replied, "I asked if you had come by the schoolhouse on your way. I wondered if you had seen it yet."

"Oh, yes. Yes, I did. I have." Leonard hadn't mentioned my being here then. I should have been grateful, but for some reason I was annoyed with him and myself. I determined to pay attention to the conversation, and the rest of the mealtime passed uneventfully.

Very soon after supper, Pa rose to leave. I walked out to the buggy with him.

"Have a good week, Mabel," he said. "We'll be praying for you."

"Thanks, Pa. I'm sure I'll need it. This first week will probably not be easy, but I know I'm going to enjoy it." I watched the buggy out of sight.

"I won't be going to church this evening, Miss O'Dell," Mrs. Williams said. "Pa can go with Len, and Alice and I will help you get settled."

I was relieved to hear that. After this week I would probably be expected to attend evening service on Sundays, but for tonight anyway, I was spared the embarrassment of sitting in Leonard's congregation.

As soon as the dishes were cleared away, we went upstairs to my room.

"Oh, this is lovely!" I exclaimed.

"You can see the school from this window," Alice pointed out.

The crisp white curtains framed a panorama of the countryside that was breathtaking. It seemed as though I might be able to see as far as Sarah Jane's school, if there had not been so many trees covering the hills.

"There is a desk here for you," Mrs. Williams said, "but we want you to know that you are welcome to work downstairs with us. You are part of the family, and the house is yours. Now, let's get your trunk unpacked so that Len can take it out of your way."

We quickly unpacked my clothes and books.

"This room will be very comfortable in the winter, Miss O'Dell. You are over the kitchen, and the stovepipe comes right up here. It will keep you nice and warm."

"I know I'll be happy with it," I said. "But, please, call me Mabel. 'Miss O'Dell' is too formal for a family."

"All right, Mabel," she replied. "I like that better, too. Let's go down and sit on the porch until the men get home, shall we?"

I had rather hoped to be in my own room for the night before the men got home, but when we were seated outside in the cool evening, I was glad to be there.

"Do you know how many children will be in school this year," I asked Alice, "and how many grades?"

"There should be fifteen," she replied. "There are no eighth graders this fall as far as I know, but there are three in the seventh. Sixth grade has two, fifth grade has three, and second, third, and fourth each have one. Then there are four beginners."

"The Abbot twins will be starting this year, won't they?" Mrs. Williams put in. "You may have a little trouble telling them apart. Joanna and Roseanna they're named."

"They call them Josie and Rosie," Alice added. "They do look an awful lot alike."

"I'm sure it will take awhile to attach the correct name to everyone," I admitted, "but I'll work at it. Are the books all there?"

"Oh, yes," Mrs. Williams assured me. "Mr. Elliot took them over last week when he finished cleaning. He will be the janitor for the schoolhouse. The Elliots live on the next farm. It won't take you long to get acquainted with everyone."

It was dusk before Mr. Williams and Len

returned from church. Mrs. Williams went in to light the lamps, and I watched Len as he led the horse to the barn. Sarah Jane had been right; he *was* nice looking. Still, that meant nothing to me, for I was sure we would not be exchanging very many words. I certainly had nothing to say to him!

"We have family prayers before we retire at night," Mr. Williams told me. "We would be honored to have you join us."

On Monday morning I was wide awake before daybreak. As I leaned out the window, sniffing the early morning air, I was conscious of a rustling beneath me. When my eyes became accustomed to the light, I could see that the cause was the ornery goat I had met before. He was vigorously chewing on the lilac bush and would probably have it cleaned out to the roots before anyone was aware of him. Perhaps I should dress quickly and try to head him back toward the barn with the broomstick.

No, I thought, *let Leonard take care of it. It's his fault for not keeping the animal tied.* I pulled my head back in and took my time dressing and reading my Bible. When I heard a stirring in the kitchen, I went downstairs.

"You'll not be having time to help with

meals, Mabel," Mrs. Williams said, "nor is there any need to. I appreciate your offer, but your job will be as big as you'll need to keep you busy." She hurried around the kitchen as she talked. "It's going to be a nice day. I suppose you'll want to get to school early this morning, it being the opening and all."

I nodded and opened my mouth to answer, but she was still speaking.

"Len is going over with you this morning to raise the flag. You can appoint an older boy to take care of that from now on, but since we kept the flag here this summer, he'll take care of it today."

I was about to protest that I could handle it very nicely, when Len and his father came in from the barn.

"Good morning, Miss O'Dell," Len said. "I'll be ready to leave for school whenever you are."

"Really, that won't be necessary. I'm sure I can raise the flag."

"No bother at all," he replied cheerfully. "I'll be glad to see that everything is in order for you."

"Breakfast is on the table," Mrs. Williams announced. "Are you all ready for your first day?"

"I think so. I guess I'm a little nervous, but I'm excited, too."

45

"Buffer chewed the bottom off the lilac bush this morning, Ma," Len said, after Mr. Williams had said grace. "I try to keep him tied, but he's eaten through every rope we have. I don't think he ever sleeps like the other animals on the place. He spends the night gnawing through his tether. I'm sorry I didn't see him before he ruined your bush."

"So am I," Mrs. Williams replied. "Your grandmother planted that bush when she came here as a bride."

I felt a moment of regret that I hadn't done something about the goat.

"I think I have a chain in the barn we can use at night," Mr. Williams said. "It's pretty heavy to drag around, but it may put a cramp in his style."

"We'll try that tonight," Len said. "I can keep an eye on him during the day." He glanced at me. "At least most of the time I can head him off when he starts for the yard."

I blushed and busied myself with my breakfast. That aggravating man was laughing at me again! I was sorry about the lilac, but it wasn't my responsibility to look after the goat, even if I had been the only one to see him.

After morning prayers, I gathered my books and lunch pail and prepared to leave.

Len jumped up to hold the door open. "Let me carry your books for you, Miss O'Dell," he said. "You'll find this a pleasant walk in nice weather. When the roads are bad, we'll take you over in the buggy or the sleigh."

"Are you always this thoughtful of the schoolteachers?" I asked him.

"Thoughtful?" He looked surprised. "Well, actually, I've never carried their books or given them a ride. But then," he said with a grin, "you're the first lady teacher we've had here since Pa has been on the school board. Not that Pa doesn't like lady teachers," he hastened to add. "It's just that none has ever applied before."

He looked down at me carefully. "You are pretty small," he said. "I hope you won't have any problems with the big boys. If you do have trouble, don't hesitate to call me. I'll see that they're taken care of."

"Thank you. I'm sure I'll manage." *And if I can't,* I thought, *you would be way down on the list of people I'd tell about it.*

From inside the schoolhouse I could hear the noise of the children arriving. I consulted my watch and took a deep breath. It was time to open the door and ring the bell for the first day of school.

5

School
Opens

THE CHILDREN WERE GROUPED AROUND the door when I opened it, and before I could even ring the bell, they were rushing past me and into the room. The little ones were pushed aside, lunch pails clanged, and voices reverberated from wall to wall. I walked to the front and stood by my desk until everyone was seated. Since I had not yet said anything, they were soon eyeing me curiously. When it was quiet, I *did* say something.

"Good morning, boys and girls. My name is Miss O'Dell. You have come to school to learn something, and we'll begin right now. Stand, please."

The children glanced at each other. Then one by one they stood by the desks.

"Now turn around and march back out the door to the school yard."

Uncertainly they began to move. Some of the girls giggled nervously, and the boys shoved each other. I followed them outside and stood on the lower step of the porch.

"The girls will line up on the right side, from the smallest to the largest. The boys on the left in the same order."

In my mind I could hear Sarah Jane saying, "You didn't lose any time separating the sheep from the goats," and I almost laughed. This was not the occasion, however, to indulge in humor.

When two fairly straight lines faced me, I introduced these children to a new way of doing things.

"This is your first lesson this year," I told them. "We do not enter our classroom like a herd of pigs headed for the trough. When I ring the bell, you will line up as you are now. When I say good morning to you, you will have the courtesy to answer me. Good morning, boys and girls."

"Good morning, Miss O'Dell," they chorused.

"You will please find a desk in the row corresponding to your grade when we enter the room."

The little ones in the front of me looked bewildered, and I realized that they probably hadn't the faintest idea what I was talking about. I smiled at them and said, "The beginners will be in the first row at the front of the room. Shall we go in now?"

We all filed back to our desks, still in

silence. It was obvious that they were not sure what to think of this new teacher. I counted to be sure I had my full quota this first day. Fifteen. Alice had been right. And so had I, when I surmised that some of my students would be bigger than I was. One-fourth of the class was taller, including the seventh-grade girl.

"You will not be required to walk around in silence like a troop of soldiers," I said. "I simply want you to know that we will do things decently and in order, as the Bible instructs us. Now, starting with the seventh grade, will you stand and tell me your names?"

One by one I heard the names that, before the year was over, would be as familiar to me as my own: Elsie, Abe, George, Carrie, Prudence . . .

The only little boy in the beginner class could not be persuaded to lift his head, let alone his body, from his desk when it was his turn. "He's my brother, Toby," seventh grader George Elliot informed me. "He's awful bashful."

I stooped down in front of Toby's desk. "Toby Elliot? Say, is it your father who takes care of our school?" The buried head nodded. "Well, I'm glad you're here. Will you do something for me?" One eye peered up over the folded arms. "Will you tell your father when you get home how much we appreciate the nice job he did to make our room look so neat?" The other eye looked out and regarded me seriously.

Toby's head came up, and he answered loudly, "Yes, ma'am!"

There were two beginners left, the twins. I could see at once that it would not be easy to tell them apart by any physical characteristic. I would have to watch for some significant mannerism to distinguish them.

The rest of the morning was devoted to handing out books, appointing monitors, and assigning lessons.

"I don't believe those Abbot twins can tell each other apart," I said to Mrs. Williams that evening. "They change seats, and either one may answer a question, no matter which one is asked. I don't dare say anything to one without looking at both."

By Friday we were settled into a routine of sorts. I had time to pay attention to individual children, and they were beginning to behave in typical ways.

Teddy Sawyer came in from recess with an announcement. "Miss O'Dell, there ain't no dipper in the water bucket."

"There *isn't any* dipper in the water bucket," I corrected him automatically.

"Oh, I thought you didn't know." Teddy sat down.

"I didn't know until you told me," I said. "Can anyone tell us what happened to the dipper?"

"I might be able to find it," Abe Lawton spoke up from the back row. "You want I should try?"

He was grinning from ear to ear, and I was aware that he not only might be able to find it, but had probably put it wherever it was.

"Very well, Abe. You may go."

He rose cheerfully and slouched out the door. I was sure we would not be seeing him for several minutes—as long as he dared prolong his mission.

The upper grades were working on a writing assignment, and I wanted to spend some time with the middlers on arithmetic. I would need help with the beginners. The seventh graders were busy, so I scanned the sixth-grade row. Prudence Edwards looked up at me.

"Prudence, if you've finished your writing, I'd appreciate it if you could help the beginners with letters and numbers."

Prudence smiled and closed her book. She soon had the four little ones surrounding her, reciting the alphabet rhymes. I became aware that the twins were giving her a problem, too.

Josie began.

"A is for apple, so round and so red.

B is for baby, in his little bed.

C is for cat, so fluffy and light.

D is for dog, who . . ."

"Barks in the night!" Rosie supplied.

"Don't help her, Rosie," Prudence said. "She can recite by herself."

The afternoon droned to a close, and it was soon time to dismiss the children. I watched them scatter in different directions, and then turned to go back to my desk. A rustling sound at the side of the building prompted me to see who had not left with the others. It was Abe Lawton. He had not heard me approach, and I watched a moment to see what he was doing. He appeared to be trying to open a window, using a stick as a lever.

"Abe? Did you forget something?"

Startled, he faced me, his eyes wide with fear.

"No'm," he muttered. "Didn't forget nothin'."

"Then what are you doing?"

"Nothin'. Just fooling around."

"I don't think the schoolhouse is a good place to 'fool around,' " I said. "Don't you have chores to do at home?"

"Yes'm," he answered sullenly. "I'm goin' now."

As he threw down the stick and started away, the sleeve of his shirt caught on the window ledge. There was a loud rip as the seam gave way, and Abe looked at the gap in dismay.

"I'll get it now," he said. "Ma'll thrash me if Pa don't get me first."

"It's not that bad, Abe," I said. "Come on, I've got some thread in my desk. I can stitch it for you in just a minute."

Reluctantly Abe followed me back into the room, holding the shirt-sleeve in place.

"Sit down. This won't take long."

He took his hand away, and I gasped as the cloth fell to reveal ugly dark bruises on his arm and shoulder.

"Oh, Abe! Have you been fighting?"

He shook his head.

"Then where did you get these horrible marks?"

His head was down, and I thought he was not going to answer me.

"Pa whupped me," he said finally.

He 'whupped' you more than once to do that much damage, I thought to myself. I was not used to a father who manhandled his sons. I didn't know what to say.

"Does your ma know about these bruises?"

54

"She knows."

As quickly as I could, I sewed the sleeve together.

"All right, Abe. You hurry on home, and I'll see you Monday."

He left swiftly, and I sat down to think. What, if anything, should I do? I was aware that parents considered children their property, and that it would probably not be wise to question their care of them. But could I stand by silently when I knew that a boy was being physically abused? *There's nothing Abe could have done to deserve that harsh a beating,* I thought indignantly. Perhaps I should speak with Len about it. He knew the family, and could advise me.

I cleared my desk, gathered up my papers and books to take home, and glanced around the room. A copybook lay on the floor near the back, and on my way out, I picked it up. As I opened it to find where it belonged, my eye fell on a sentence at the bottom of the page.

"Elizabeth says Miss O. has her cap set for Leonard Williams."

Julie Ann Lawton was the name on it, and my face felt hot as I shoved the book into her desk. I left as quickly as I could, locking the door behind me. Hurrying down the road toward the Williams house, I was thankful that I would be heading toward my own dear home in just a short while.

I was looking forward eagerly to the two days at home, and I was sure that would never be enough time to tell Sarah Jane about my week, and to hear about hers.

As I walked, I thought about the scribbled comment. Set my cap, indeed! Mr. Lawton whipped the wrong child, I thought angrily, and then immediately felt remorse. No child deserved that kind of treatment, not even one who spread horrid tales. My face grew warm again, and I slowed my steps. I could not confide in Len now. I must be careful to avoid him as much as possible. I certainly would not give anyone in this community an opportunity to spread stories.

Len and Alice were in the kitchen when I arrived. I had hoped to have my things together and be gone before he came in from his work.

"Would you ladies like to see what Pa and I brought home this afternoon?" Len asked us. "It's out in the barn."

"Oh, yes!" Alice dropped the sewing she was doing on the table. "What is it?"

I couldn't very well refuse without being impolite, so I put my books down and followed after them.

"Buffer is chained," Len told me. "He won't

get in our way." He didn't appear to be laughing at me, but I couldn't be sure.

We entered the barn, and Alice ran to a stall in the back. "A roan horse!" she exclaimed. "Len, is he yours? What's his name?"

"He doesn't have one yet," Len replied. "I thought maybe Miss O'Dell would help us name him." He looked at me questioningly.

"Oh, he's beautiful!" I stroked the horse's chestnut-colored coat which was thickly peppered with gray. He stamped impatiently.

It was obvious that this was not a workhorse. Len put a bridle on him and led him outside.

"Won't he look great pulling the buggy?" he exclaimed boyishly.

"Indeed he will," I said. "I've never seen a more handsome horse. He needs a special name."

"That is why I thought you should suggest something," Len said.

"I'll think about it," I replied. "I'm sure we can come up with a name." As Len led the horse back into the barn, I thought of Nellie, the faithful old puller of buggies that we had loved for so many years. I didn't remember who had named her, but it was probably my oldest brother, Reuben. He had a special empathy with all our animals.

I had only a few minutes before it was time to go home, so I hurried to gather what I needed to take with me. As I looked out my window toward the school, I realized that I loved my job. It had been a good week in spite of today's misfortunes, and whatever lay ahead I could handle, with the help of the Lord.

"Mabel! Your friends are here!" Alice called up the stairs.

I rushed down and hugged Sarah Jane.

"I see you haven't aged a great deal since I left you," she said. "Were you a great success?"

"It's too soon to tell," I replied. "At least they haven't told me not to come back. Oh, I'm sorry. I didn't introduce you to my 'family' while I'm here. Mr. and Mrs. Williams. Their niece, Alice, and ... Leonard Williams." I glanced at Sarah Jane sharply. A look of surprise crossed her face, and her eyes lit up mischievously. But all she said was, "How do you do?"

"So that's the hired man!" she snorted as we drove out the gate. "Has he said anything about your grand entrance?"

"Of course not," I answered primly, "and it's time you forgot about it, too."

"I may not talk about it, but it will be a

long time before I can forget it," she replied. "Now, tell me all about your week."

We chattered nonstop all the way home, causing Mr. Clark to declare that his ears were sore by the time he let me off at our porch. Sarah Jane promised to come back after supper, and I ran up the steps to greet Ma.

It was so good to be home! We had a nice visit while we ate. When we were doing the dishes, I told Ma about the new horse. "Regal!" I said. "That's what he should be called."

"Is it your place to name him?" Ma inquired.

"Well, yes, Len said that I could." My cheeks got a little warm. "Of course, I'll just suggest it. It will be his choice, really."

"I'm glad you've had a successful beginning, Mabel. Let's go out and sit with Pa until Sarah Jane gets here, shall we? I want to hear about her school, too."

I sat down on the steps, took a deep breath, and leaned against the post. There were so many new things to think about!

6

The Problems Start

Miss O'Dell, Edward is grabbing our rope again. We're trying to jump, and he won't let us."

I walked out to the playground to see what was going on.

"Edward, if you want to play with the girls' rope, suppose you help swing it for them to jump."

Edward looked at me with horror, but I put one end of the rope in his hand and took the other end myself. After every girl had a chance to jump, I gave the rope back to them, and put my arm around Edward's shoulder.

"Why aren't you playing stickball with the boys?" I asked. "Wouldn't that be better than interfering with the girls?"

"They don't want me to play."

"Why not? You know the rules, don't you?"

He nodded. "But they say I have to do it like they do, and I can't 'cause I'm a lefty. They say I do everything backwards." He looked at me imploringly. "I try to use my right hand, Miss O'Dell, I really do. But it just won't work the way the left one does."

"Of course it won't," I agreed. "The other boys can't work with their left hands as well, either. I have an idea that may help you out. We'll talk about it when recess is over."

I went back into the room and took out my Bible. If I could find the Scripture I needed, it would be a good lesson. By the time the children filed back in, I was ready.

"We have something for everyone to do together," I announced. "The beginners need help with their counting, so we'll start with them. Nancy, how many people in our room have brown hair?"

Nancy stood importantly and counted. "Eight," she reported.

"Now, Toby, can you write eight on the board?"

He did, and then I asked, "Josie, how many people have blonde hair, like yours?"

"Seven."

Toby wrote seven on the board.

"Ted, how many is that?"

"Fifteen."

"But there are sixteen of us in the room. Was someone forgotten?"

"Me," Joel Gage answered. "No one counted me."

"Oh, but your hair is red, Joel. You don't fit in one of these groups, do you?"

"I'm the only one with red hair here," Joel bristled, "but I'm not the only one in the world."

"You certainly aren't," I told him. "There are many people with beautiful red hair like yours. Why do you suppose God made us all different?"

"So he wouldn't get us mixed up," Jamie suggested.

"Because he likes different colors," Carrie said.

"So we'd look like our folks," Joel guessed.

"Those are good reasons," I nodded. "God uses us for different things, too. He doesn't choose us for how we look, but he often chooses people for what they can do. I found a story in the Bible that you may not have heard. You know that in the time of David, men often fought wars with swords and stones. In one battle, they had some special men. 'Among all these soldiers there were seven hundred chosen men who were *left-handed*, each of whom could sling a stone at a hair and not miss.' What do you think of that?"

Edward beamed, and the rest of the boys had the grace to look sheepish.

"Can I copy that down and show it to my pa?" Edward asked. "He'll like that!"

"Of course," I said. "That can be your

writing lesson for today. Now, everyone get books out and finish the morning lessons."

As I looked at the heads bent busily over their work, I thought of the list of "crimes" I had found in my desk, along with appropriate penalties.

telling lies .... 2 lashes
blotting your copybook .... 2 lashes
fighting on the school ground. 10 lashes
fighting on the way home ..... 5 lashes
using bad language............ 8 lashes

I was sure the former teacher thought he was doing me a favor by letting me know the procedures for discipline, but I shuddered to think of using a switch on any child. Surely there were better ways to exact obedience!

The kitchen was warm and smelled like fresh bread when I arrived home in the late afternoon.

"Mm, smells good," I sniffed appreciatively. "Is that bean soup on the stove?"

"Yes, I thought it sounded like a perfect fall supper," Mrs. Williams replied. "And it's easy to fix on washday. How was school?"

"It was fine. I think we'll just have to take a trip to the woods one of these days to start collecting leaves. The colors are so gorgeous, and just what the upper grades need for their biology notebook projects."

"By the time you have your clothes changed, we can eat," Mrs. Williams told me. "I just saw Pa and Len go into the barn."

As we finished getting the table ready, they walked through the door. While Len washed for supper, he said, "I was fixing the fence on the back hill this afternoon, and I saw you leave the schoolhouse. Just a few minutes later, I noticed someone down there. Whoever it was disappeared around the corner before I could tell whether it was a boy or a girl. Did you leave someone at school when you came home?"

"No," I replied. "I was the last to go. I wonder who it could have been? All the children left at least a half hour before I did."

"I'll walk down after supper and check it out," Len offered. "I can't imagine anyone hanging around school just for the fun of it."

"Neither can I," I replied. "And I can't think of anyone who would come back for any other reason." The picture of Abe poking at the window crossed my mind, but I dismissed it. Surely he wouldn't have stayed around after last week's encounter.

During supper Mrs. Williams told us that there was to be a quilting party at the Gages' home a week from Saturday.

"I think you would enjoy it, Mabel," Alice said. "It would be a chance to meet all the families in the area."

"We take our dinner, and the men come to eat at noon," Mrs. Williams added. "I know that the ladies will enjoy getting acquainted with you. Do you think you could plan to stay?"

They were obviously anxious to have me, and though I would have preferred to go home, I agreed.

"I'd like to know all the parents of my children," I said. "And that would be a good opportunity. But I'm not sure Mrs. Gage will want my 'hen tracks' on her quilt. That's what Sarah Jane calls my stitching."

Mrs. Williams laughed. "The variety of stitches on a quilt is what makes it unique. I'm sure yours aren't as bad as all that."

After prayers, Len and Mr. Williams started out for the school, and I brought my books to the table. The evening had turned cool, and the kitchen was a cozy place to work. The smell of fresh bread lingered in the air, and the fire crackled in the cookstove. Alice sat down opposite me with her sewing.

I sighed over my papers. "I see that Carrie Lawton has given the upper peninsula of Michigan away again. I do wish she had a better eye for a map."

"Well, the upper peninsula *is* attached to Wisconsin and it doesn't touch the rest of

Michigan," Alice commented. "It does look as though it might belong to them."

"It was Congress that made that decision, in 1836," I answered, unable to resist the opportunity to teach. "Michigan and Ohio both wanted the strip of land that included the city of Toledo. So Congress let Ohio have the Toledo strip, and in exchange, Michigan received the upper peninsula."

"I'm not sure we didn't get the best of that bargain," Alice commented. "It's certainly a lot more territory."

I went back to my maps, and as I worked I thought of the students whose names were on these papers.

Abe Lawton. I knew he was the only boy in a family of girls, and as such felt entitled to be boss of the clan. That his responsibility didn't include the whole school had never occurred to him. He was loud, rude, unkempt and rough, but so far he had not given me any trouble; he was just a minor irritant. His sister Carrie was the same grade, though she was a year younger. Julie Ann was two years younger, and Nancy, a beginner.

George Elliot was shy and quiet, as were his younger brothers, Jamie and Toby. They were no problem at all. I had to remind myself to pay attention to them.

There were two girls in the sixth grade:

Elsie Mathews and Prudence Edwards. Prudence was pleasant and cheerful, and Elsie was the direct opposite. I thought she looked petulant and haughty at the same time, if that is possible. She declined to enter into our conversations at dinnertime and did the tasks assigned to her with an air of disdain. Elsie had no particular friend that I could see, unless it might have been Julie Ann Lawton, who was her faithful worshiper.

The only other pupil in the upper grades was Joel Gage, the son of the storekeeper in town. Joel reminded me of Warren Carter, because he was an exceptionally good student.

By the time I had finished grading geography maps, Len and Mr. Williams had returned.

"I was right about someone being at school," Len said. "The back door was pried open."

"Oh, no! Was anything taken?"

"I couldn't see that it was," he replied. "Of course, I don't know what you had in your desk, but nothing looked as though it had been disturbed. Do you think one of your students could have broken in?"

I opened my mouth to tell him about Abe, and then closed it again and shook my head.

"I wouldn't want to suspect any of them," I said. "I can't think why anyone would want to get in, unless they forgot something. Even then, they could have come to me. I'll keep my ears open tomorrow. Someone may know something, and if they know, they won't be able to keep it quiet!"

Len started upstairs and then turned back. "Oh, you had some mail today, and I forgot to give it to you." He placed the envelope in front of me and left abruptly. The return address read, "Russ Bradley, Ann Arbor, Michigan."

I slipped the letter under my books, but not before Alice had seen the name.

"Oh, that's from your boyfriend, isn't it? Is he studying at the university? Aren't you going to read it?"

I nodded. "Three of the boys from my class are there this year. Russ is probably just telling me what they are doing." I blushed. "I'm sure it isn't important. It will wait till I've finished my lessons."

Alice said no more, and I was silently thankful that she was not like Sarah Jane. *She* would have made sure that the letter was not only opened, but read to her in its entirety.

Good old Sarah Jane! How I needed her to confide in right now. She would know whether I ought to tell someone about Abe's problems, and whether I should confront Julie Ann on the subject of gossiping. I would talk it over with her this weekend, but in the meantime, there were lessons to prepare for tomorrow.

It was nearly nine o'clock when I finally closed my books and gathered my papers together. Alice put her sewing in the basket and rose, too.

"It's nice to have someone to work with in the evening," she said. "Even when we don't talk a lot, it's good company."

I agreed. "I'm sure I'll have more time to visit when I get this teaching business learned a little better. I'm anxious to hear about your wedding plans and where you're going to live."

Alice lit another lamp, and I carried the one from the table with me. I was tired, and worried, too. If one of my students had broken into the school, what kind of punishment should I mete out? This was a serious offense, and the culprit should know he had been punished.

When I dropped my books on the desk, Russ's letter fluttered to the floor. I could hear Sarah Jane's indignant voice. *You forgot it! Mabel, when someone cares enough about you to write you, you might at least take time to read it! Sometimes I really despair of you!"*

I sat down on the bed and opened the envelope.

Dear Mabel,
Thomas, Warren, and I are all settled in and ready to begin classes. I have a pretty heavy schedule, but I'm looking forward to it. In spite of his jibes at you, I think Warren feels a little bad that you didn't get the scholarship. He thinks he could have worked and kept up his studies. Of course I wish you had, too. It would be much pleasanter here if I could see you every day. Warren is a good fellow, but he's not much to look at! We've already decided that I'll go home with him at Thanksgiving time, so may I come to see you then?

Please write and tell me how your school is going and what you are doing to keep busy. Say hello to Sarah Jane for me. I think Thomas has already written to her.

Yours truly,
Russ

I sighed and put the letter away. My school days seemed far behind me just now, though it hadn't been four months since we graduated. I wondered if teaching was going to make an old person out of me the first year.

7

Mr. Lawton's
Threats

I'D LIKE TO GET TO SCHOOL EARLY THIS morning," I said at breakfast. "I'm anxious to see that everything is all right."

"Your dinner is packed," Mrs. Williams said. "You can leave anytime you're ready. I'm sure Len would go over with you if you're fearful."

"Oh, I'm not at all worried about anyone being there. I just want to be sure the school is in good order and nothing is missing."

I hurried to be on my way before Len could return from the barn and insist on accompanying me. I had to admit that I would have enjoyed having him along, but I would certainly never let any of my children or their parents see me with Leonard Williams. They must think I was awfully anxious to get married if I would pursue the first young man I met! Let Elizabeth—whoever she was—do the chasing.

I was not the first to arrive. Elsie Mathews was sitting on the school steps, and got up when I came through the gate.

"Good morning, Miss O'Dell," she said politely. "Isn't this a beautiful day?"

I eyed her with suspicion. Elsie had not gone out of her way to be pleasant to me, nor anyone else, as far as I had observed.

"Yes, it is beautiful," I agreed. "Autumn is one of my favorite seasons. You're here pretty early this morning, aren't you?"

"It was so nice outside that I just decided to leave earlier than usual."

There was obviously no more information than that forthcoming, so I went on into the room. Just as Len had said, there appeared to be nothing out of place. As I wrote assignments on the board and arranged the lessons for the day, I found myself wondering what *had* brought Elsie to school so early. Perhaps I should have taken time to talk to her. Maybe there was something she wanted to tell me. But no, I decided, Elsie was not the confiding type. It was probably just as she had said. It was a beautiful morning.

There were still several minutes until time to ring the bell, so I went outside to stand in the sun. Prudence and George were talking, and Elsie stood alone by the gate. I wondered if any of them knew about last night's activities, but decided I would not question them until I had learned what I could by watching and listening quietly. I rang the

72

bell, and the day began.

As soon as everyone was in his seat, we sang a hymn and had prayer as usual. When I took the roll, neither Carrie nor Abe Lawton was there. I questioned Julie Ann about their absence.

"Carrie had to stay home to help Ma today," she replied.

"Is Abe going to be late, then?"

"No'm. I don't think so."

"Is he sick?"

"No'm. I don't think so."

"Well, what *do* you think?"

"I think he runned away, Miss O'Dell."

"You think he *ran* away," I corrected her, and then hastily I added, "all right, Julie Ann. We'll talk about it later. Open your books, please."

Had Abe been in here last night? And if so, what for? I reprimanded myself for being so suspicious and gave out assignments. The upper grades began work on arithmetic, and I settled down to hear the younger children read. I half listened as they droned on. When I glanced up at the others from time to time, it appeared to me that they were having difficulty concentrating. Elsie seemed uneasy, and Joel, who is usually most interested in mathematics, spent a lot of time staring into space and chewing on his pencil.

Prudence looked out the window and made two trips to the water bucket. Only George Elliot gave his full attention to the arithmetic book and seemed oblivious to what was going on around him.

When it was time for them to recite, I called Elsie to put her work on the board first.

"You've copied the problem incorrectly from your book, Elsie," I told her. "Copy it over and do it again, please. Prudence, do you have that one?"

Prudence put her work on the board. The problem was right, but the answer was wrong. I was beginning to feel impatient.

"What are you all thinking about this morning?" I asked. "Your minds certainly aren't on mathematics. Joel, will you work it for us?"

Joel was staring out the window and didn't respond.

"Joel?"

He jumped and looked embarrassed.

"Yes, ma'am? I'm sorry, I didn't hear you."

"I asked if you'd put the first problem on the board for us. Your lesson is done, isn't it?"

"Yes, ma'am. Er, no, ma'am. I mean, not completely. Well, I guess I was just thinking about something else."

I sighed. "Yes, I guess you were. This does not promise to be a very productive day. All of you copy your lesson on paper and hand it in. I'll get back to you later."

It was a relief when ten-thirty arrived, and everyone headed for the school ground. The smaller children trotted off to play their games, while most of the others surrounded Julie Ann.

"Did Abe really run away from home, Julie?"

She nodded, pleased to be the center of so much attention.

"Where did he go?"

"I don't know. Maybe to town or somewhere."

"What'd he run away for? Did he get into trouble?"

Julie Ann appeared uncertain. "Pa switched him, I guess. I don't know what for."

This was not as informative as everyone had hoped, and they soon drifted off, leaving Julie Ann with her own friends.

I, too, was concerned about Abe's absence. It may have been a personal matter that had brought him another beating and sent him away from home, but there seemed to be too much coincidence between the break-in and his disappearance. I hoped I was making more of it than was really there.

When the children filed back in after recess, I announced, "I have decided that we'll take our lunches and go to the woods. This will be a good day to finish your nature study projects."

Joel's head jerked up, and his face turned first red and then white. "Miss O'Dell," he said, "may I please be excused?"

I was surprised, but I said, "Of course, Joel."

He left the room hurriedly, and I continued my instructions. By the time we had collected lunches and biology material and were ready to leave, he was back, panting heavily. I had no time to wonder where he had been, since getting the little ones in line and starting out was a full-time endeavor.

The boys ran on ahead, and Prudence, Julie Ann, and Hannah Sawyer walked together. Elsie straggled along behind them, and I brought up the rear with the beginners.

Amid much chattering, we finally reached a shady grove and sat down on a log to eat our lunches. The leaves were especially beautiful this year, it seemed, and the children spread out to collect the prettiest of them.

Time passed quickly and I was surprised to

see that the sun had gone under a cloud. "It looks as though it might storm, children. We'd better start back. Be sure you don't leave anything behind."

We returned more quickly than we had come, and reached the schoolhouse just as large raindrops began to fall. Since there were only a few minutes left before dismissal time, I sent everyone on home.

Len had offered to take me over to Edanville after school to see Sarah Jane, and Alice had been pleased with an invitation to ride along. There was still time to get some work done before time to leave. I erased the board and began writing tomorrow's assignments. As I worked, the door opened, and someone entered the room. One of the children, I assumed.

"Did you forget something?" I asked without turning around.

No one answered, so I looked over my shoulder. In front of my desk stood a large, rough-looking man. I had never seen him before, but he resembled Abe so closely that I knew at once it was Mr. Lawton.

"Well, well. You *are* a pretty little thing." He stared at me admiringly, and I moved a little closer to the desk.

"Is there something I can do for you, Mr. Lawton?" I was surprised to hear that my voice sounded normal, because I was frightened almost out of my wits.

"No sense in bein' formal, Miss. You an' me can be real good friends," he said smoothly.

The thought crossed my mind that I would rather befriend a rattlesnake, but I said nothing. That seemed to disconcert him, and his look changed to belligerence.

"I come to see why Abe ain't home from school," he said harshly. "You keep him in to punish him?"

I shook my head. "Abe wasn't in school today, Mr Lawton."

"And I s'pose you're going to tell me you don't know where he is."

"No, I don't."

"I don't believe that," Mr. Lawton snarled, moving closer to the desk. "His ma told me how you mended his shirt. No teacher never took no interest in that kid before. You know where he is all right, and you'd better tell me." He advanced menacingly and grabbed my wrist.

Just at that moment Elsie Mathews opened the door and came in. I had never been so glad to see her. As she stood and gazed curiously at us, Mr. Lawton dropped his hand and backed away.

"You'll be seeing more of me, Miss Schoolmarm," he said. Brushing past Elsie, he departed hurriedly.

I sank into my chair, weak and shaking.

"I forgot my copybook, Miss O'Dell," Elsie was saying. "I need it to finish my lesson tonight."

"Good," I replied. "I'm glad you did." I ignored the perplexed look on the girl's face. "If you'll wait a minute until I clear my desk, I'll walk with you."

As quickly as I could, I secured the windows and locked the big front door. The rain had slackened, and we turned toward home. A glance around showed no sign of Mr. Lawton, but I was thankful for Elsie's company as far as her road. She said nothing, nor did I. It would do no good to try to explain what she had seen, and besides, I had no explanation for it myself.

My heart had returned to its accustomed place, and I'd regained most of my composure by the time I arrived home. Then I began to feel angry. How dare that man come into my school and threaten me? Should I tell someone about it?

Perhaps I could confide in Alice. She might know what to do. On further thought, however, I decided that might not be wise. Alice would feel obliged to tell Mr. Williams, and he would think it necessary to confront Mr.

Lawton. I already knew of that man's uncertain temper, and I didn't want Mr. Williams on the receiving end of it. And telling Len was out of the question. How many more things was I going to be forced to keep to myself? If all this is included in being on one's own, it was harder than I had thought it would be.

Len was ready when I got home, and the trip to Edanville was pleasant, even though my thoughts were in a turmoil. Sarah Jane was glad to see us, and we visited for about an hour. There was no opportunity to speak with her alone, but as we were leaving, she grinned at me.

"You'd better make lemonade or something for the ladies while they quilt next Saturday, Mabel. You know what you can do to a piece of cloth with a needle. You need me to keep an eye on you."

"Don't worry, Sarah Jane," I told her. "Five miles isn't enough distance to separate us. I feel you looking over my shoulder every day. But thanks for the advice."

She waved to us, and we turned toward the road. We arrived home just in time for supper.

"That was a quick trip," Mrs. Williams said. "I wouldn't have been surprised if you hadn't gotten home before dark."

"Regal is a good horse," Len told her. "He doesn't waste time thinking it over when he wants to go someplace."

"Do you think your friend Sarah Jane would like to come for the quilting?" Mrs. Williams asked as we ate. "The ladies would be happy to include her, and we'd be pleased to have her stay here."

"I'll suggest it to her this weekend," I answered. "I'd like that, and I think she would, too. Thank you for thinking of it."

I lay awake a long time that night, listening to the rain on the roof and thinking about the events of the day. I concluded that I must leave everything in the Lord's hands and trust him to work it out. That course of action had never failed in the past, and it surely would not fail now.

8

Joel Solves
One Mystery

Y OU HAVE ANOTHER LETTER FROM YOUR young man in Ann Arbor," Mrs. Williams informed me when I returned from school several days later. "Len put it on the table for you." She glanced at me. "He seems to be quite interested in you."

I knew she meant Russ, not Len.

"He's just a friend. There are a number of students from our class in Ann Arbor." I was flustered, and annoyed with myself for showing it. After all, Russ didn't mean anything special to me. Why did everyone persist in thinking he did?

It was becoming obvious by his letters, however, that Russ didn't share my views on the subject. I had told him that he was welcome to call at Thanksgiving time, and his reply left me feeling a bit uneasy:

I look forward to seeing you next month, and I hope we'll have time for a nice, long talk. I have something important to discuss with you. I don't think it's too soon to talk about our future, do you?

I had already thought about my future, and as far as I was concerned, it didn't include Russ or any other young man, except as friends. I would need to think of some way to get this across to him when he came.

I sighed as I put the letter down. Here was a situation I couldn't even talk over with Sarah Jane, as I already knew what her opinion would be. Of course I should encourage Russ's attentions. Did I want to grow old going to school day after day?

I pushed aside the nagging little problem and changed my clothes. There was time to grade some papers before supper. I spread my books on the desk and was absorbed in reading the day's compositions when Alice called to me.

"Mabel, one of your pupils is here to see you."

I went downstairs and found Elsie Mathews standing awkwardly by the table. "I forgot to hand in my paper, Miss O'Dell," she said. "I ran back to school with it, but you were gone."

"Thank you, Elsie. It was good of you to bring it." I waited for her to leave, but she made no move toward the door. "Was there something else you needed?"

Her eyes looked furtively around the room and then she nodded.

"I wanted to tell you that I saw Mr. Lawton going around the schoolhouse."

I was startled, but I answered calmly. "Perhaps he was looking for Abe. Did he say anything to you?"

Elsie shook her head. "He didn't see me." She hesitated again and then spoke. "I think Joel Gage knows where Abe is. You remember the day Julie Ann said he ran away?"

I nodded.

"Well, I saw Abe and Joel the night before, and I heard Abe say that Joel wasn't to tell, or he'd be sorry."

"Tell what?" I asked.

Elsie shrugged. "I don't know. I didn't hear any more. The next day, Abe was gone."

"Thank you for telling me, Elsie. Let's just keep it between us, shall we?"

Elsie nodded, and I watched her cross the yard and start toward home. What an odd child she was, I thought. She saw most everything that went on, but what she thought about it, she kept to herself.

I returned to my room, but the papers lay unnoticed on my desk. I may not have shown it before Elsie, but I was anything but calm about the news she had brought. I was particularly disturbed about Mr. Lawton's reappearance at the school. Abe had not yet returned to class, but it hadn't occurred to me that he had not come home either. Did Mr. Lawton still think I knew where Abe was? I determined to leave the schoolhouse with the children each day, and walk with them as far as possible. I would not give Mr. Lawton another chance to confront me alone.

A sudden clap of thunder brought me to my feet, and I hurried to help Alice and Mrs. Williams close the windows.

"Now that's a real downpour!" Mr. Williams exclaimed as he dripped into the kitchen. "We can surely use it." He glanced at the table. "Aren't we having supper tonight?"

"It's only four-thirty, John. You never believe there's any food unless the table's set, do you?" Mrs. Williams grumbled good-naturedly. "Get out of your wet things and sit a spell. It'll do you good to relax."

It rained hard all night, and I dodged mud puddles on the way to school the next morning. *The little ones are going to be wet to their knees,* I thought. *There's nothing they like better than a good puddle of rain.*

As soon as I entered the building, I spotted the water on the floor.

"Oh, no!" I exclaimed with exasperation. "Don't tell me we have a leak in the roof!" I ran to the corner where a pool of water stood, and looked up at the ceiling.

It didn't come from the roof, I decided. It had come in the window. But how could that have happened? On closer inspection, the window proved to be open just a crack. It was hardly enough to notice, but it had been enough for the rain to pound in.

"Someone has been in here again," I declared in exasperation to the empty room. "I *know* I closed these windows last night."

I looked around quickly but nothing appeared to have been disturbed. Except for the wet floor, everything was the way I had left it the afternoon before.

Well, I thought, *I'm going to have to straighten this out. And I believe I'll start with Joel Gage.*

When the water had been mopped up, it was time for the bell to ring. The little ones, wet to the knees as I had predicted, slogged in and put their things away. It was too early for a fire in the stove, and I hoped they wouldn't catch their deaths of foolishness before they dried out.

All the children were settled in their seats, ready to begin the day, when suddenly Abe walked in! He looked sullen and unhappy, but he sat down without a word. Joel ducked his head into his desk, pretending to look for something. No one else glanced up or acknowledged Abe's presence.

"Good morning, Abe. I'm glad you're back." I'm sure I looked as surprised as I felt.

"Yes, ma'am," he replied.

He had nothing more to say, so I called the school together and had prayer. Because this was Friday, the opening exercises took longer than usual. In addition to the hymn and Bible reading, I called on the children to recite poems and Scripture verses they had learned during the week. Nearly everyone had something to contribute, and it was almost an hour later when we got down to work.

While the upper grades wrote their history test, the middle grades worked on times tables. To the tune of "Yankee Doodle" we sang, "five times five is twenty-five, and five times six is thirty." It was necessary to adjust the time of the music in some places, but the children loved to sing, and I felt they learned faster that way. Even the beginners sang along as they did their own lessons. When we had finished, Edward begged for some mental arithmetic.

"All right," I said. "Here's one for you. If Hannah brought three apples to school, and Ted brought five apples, and they each gave away two, how many apples would they have left between them?"

Edward closed his eyes tightly and

scrunched his face up while he counted to himself. "Four!" he shouted. "They'd have four!"

"That's right," I said. "Now, Hannah, can you do this one? What is the difference between twice twenty-five and twice five and twenty?"

Hannah thought hard. "I'll have to write that down, Miss O'Dell," she said.

"All right. Put it on the board, and we'll all help you."

Hannah went to the board and wrote, "twice twenty-five is fifty." Then she turned and looked at me.

"What next?" I prompted her. "What is twice five?"

She wrote a ten.

"You remember that the word 'and' means plus? How much is ten plus twenty?"

"Thirty," she replied. "Is that the answer?"

"Not quite," I said. "The problem asked what is the difference between those two numbers. What do you do to get the difference?"

"Subtract," Ted informed her. "Take the thirty away from fifty."

"Twenty," she said when she had finished. "Is that right now?"

"Yes, indeed," I said. "You did very well. I think you could have done it even without your brother's help." I smiled at Ted, and he lowered his head, embarrassed. "It's time for recess now, so clear off your desks and get ready to go outside.

"You may hand in your history papers," I told the older students. "Go out and enjoy the beautiful weather while we have it. And, Joel, I'd like to see you before you leave, please."

When the other children had gone out, I asked him, "Joel, can you tell me anything about someone coming into the school last night or before?"

"I didn't break in, Miss O'Dell," he protested.

"That wasn't what I asked you. Can you tell me anything about it?"

Joel hung his head. "I'll get in trouble if I tell."

"I'm afraid you'll be in trouble if you don't. We need to get to the bottom of this, Joel. I'd hate to go to your parents about it if we can settle it ourselves."

Joel turned pale; then he began. "You know Julie Ann said that Abe ran away Wednesday afternoon. Well, he came over to my place. He said his pa whipped him for something he didn't do, and I had to help him, or else."

I nodded. I was sure that Abe was more

bluster than anything, but Joel was sufficiently convinced to do what Abe demanded.

"He said I should pry open the door in the back so he could sleep in the schoolhouse that night," Joel continued. "But he was in the woods when he saw Mr. Williams come down to investigate. That scared him, so he stayed where he was until I brought him some food in the morning."

Joel hesitated, and I said, "Have you told me everything?"

He shook his head. "No, ma'am. When you said we were going to the woods, I had to run and warn him. Then he told me I had to open a window for him before I left school yesterday. And that's all I know. I didn't even know he was coming back to school today."

"All right, Joel," I said. "Thank you for being truthful. I'll take care of it now. Let's not say anything to the others, shall we? I'll not tell Abe that you said anything to me."

"Oh, I won't tell anyone, Miss O'Dell. I won't say a word."

I was sure he wouldn't. Joel didn't want any more conflict with Abe Lawton.

I discussed all the things that had happened that week with Sarah Jane on Saturday as we picked up windfalls in the orchard and looked for early nuts.

90

"I think you should tell someone about Mr. Lawton," she informed me. "He could be dangerous to your health."

"I don't think so," I replied. "Abe is back home now, so there's no reason for his father to come to school. I just hope I never have a reason to keep Abe in."

"You mean you'd make Abe stay after school, knowing that that man might come back?" Sarah Jane looked at me in amazement.

"Of course," I said, "if it were necessary. I'm not going to let Mr. Lawton or any other parent tell me how to run my school!" But I wasn't at all as brave as I sounded, and Sarah Jane knew it.

"Hah!" she snorted. "I don't believe you'd keep him in for anything less than burning the schoolhouse down. If I were you, I'd ask Len to meet me after school and walk home with me."

"You wouldn't if you had nosey little girls writing notes about you," I retorted. "Who knows how many people in the neighborhood are talking about me behind my back?"

"You're not going to let anyone run your school, but you'll allow the town gossips to run your life—is that it?"

"You know better than that," I said. "Besides, Len has no interest in me. He knows that Russ is my—" I stopped. I hadn't intended to say anything like that.

"Your what?" Sarah Jane demanded. "Are you keeping something from me?"

"Don't be silly, Sarah Jane. You know better than that, too. I told you Russ was coming to see me at Thanksgiving time."

Sarah Jane planted herself in front of me and looked me squarely in the eye.

"You have never been able to deceive me in your whole life, Mabel O'Dell. What *didn't* you tell me?"

"That Russ wants to talk about our future," I said lamely.

Sarah Jane dropped down on the ground, and I sat down beside her.

"This is serious, Mabel. I have the disturbing premonition that you are going to tell him there is no future. Why do I think that?"

"Because it's probably true," I answered. "Oh, I don't know, Sarah Jane. I don't want to think about it."

"Not thinking about it won't make it go away," she reminded me. "You could hardly find a better fellow anywhere. Unless," she added eyeing me sharply, "you really *are* interested in Leonard Williams."

I denied it vehemently, but something in the back of my mind told me that Sarah Jane saw me better than I saw myself.

9

The Rotten Apples

SARAH JANE WAS PLEASED WITH THE invitation to come for the weekend and attend the quilting bee.

"There is absolutely no one my age to talk to all week long," she said. "I'm either conversing with infants or old folks. Sometimes I think there's not much difference between them."

"Some of your students are almost as old as you are," I reminded her. "Don't you talk to them?"

"I end up talking *at* them, not to them," she replied. "Besides, the things that come up in conversation at school aren't high on my interest list. It will be fun to visit for two days without correcting someone's grammar."

She arrived Friday afternoon, and we had time for a walk before supper.

"Oh, this is so much fun!" I exclaimed. "It's just like being young again. No worries or cares . . ."

"Mabel," Sarah Jane interrupted me, "we

are young. And when did we not have worries and cares of some kind?"

"You know what I mean," I replied. "Compared to what I have now, our childhood was one long summer day."

She nodded. "I guess I know what you mean. No one is responsible for making our decisions but ourselves. We are the adult population, whether we like it or not."

We walked along quietly for a moment, and then Sarah Jane asked, "Did Abe come to school all this week?"

"Yes, he was there. At least, his body was. I have a feeling that things haven't improved between him and his father. I haven't noticed any more bruises, but the girls say he gets whipped pretty regularly."

"The man ought to be reported," Sarah Jane said. "Has he stayed away from school?"

"He hasn't come into the room, but several times I've seen him watching the playground, or just leaning against a tree and staring at the schoolhouse. He makes me nervous," I admitted, "but I don't want to confront him. He may be just checking up on Abe."

Sarah Jane's expression said she didn't believe that for one single minute. To be truthful, neither did I.

94

Friday evening passed quickly and happily. We played games, popped corn, and sang around the organ while Mrs. Williams played. When we were getting ready for bed, Sarah Jane made a surprising observation.

"Some girls don't have even one young man interested in them, and you have *two* men falling at your feet. Do you think that's a fair and equitable arrangement?"

I looked at her blankly. "Two men?"

"Why, yes. Russ and Len."

"Sarah Jane! Have you taken leave of your senses? Len doesn't even know I'm alive! As far as he's concerned, I'm just like his cousin Alice."

"That's where you're mistaken, Mabel," Sarah Jane replied. "Len is crazy about you. I don't know why you haven't seen it."

"There's nothing to see," I scoffed. "I hardly ever talk to him unless the whole family is around." *And,* I thought, *that's the way it's going to stay. I won't give anyone a chance to gossip about either one of us.*

Saturday morning dawned clear and cool, a perfect late October day. We were up early to get ready for the quilting bee.

"You have enough food ready to feed the whole community," Mr. Williams remarked. "Are you ladies planning on eating all that?"

"You know we aren't, John," Mrs. Williams replied. "The menfolk will be there at noon, and food disappears when they show up."

As soon as we finished prayer and the breakfast dishes were done, Len brought the buggy around. The food was put in, and we were ready to leave. It took only a few minutes to get to the Gages' and carry our baskets into the house. Len went back to work, planning to return with the other men and boys for dinner.

I had never been in the Gage house, and I looked around with interest. It had been built the year Michigan became a state— 1837. It looked much the same as most farmhouses, but the kitchen had a big walk-in fireplace that the others didn't have. Mr. Gage's grandfather had said he couldn't live in a house that had nothing but a cookstove in the kitchen. Mrs. Gage had been heard to say that 'That was because he never had to cook in it, keep the fire going in it, or clean up after it.' Nevertheless, she admitted that the room wouldn't be the same without a fire in the winter.

Next to the kitchen was a large living room. The two rooms were separated by a big double door that was folded back so they became one large area. There was a real holiday spirit as the ladies arrived and placed their food on the pine table that had extra leaves in for the occasion.

"I thought we might like to eat outside this noon," Mrs. Gage said to Mrs. Williams. "We'll see what it's like when the men get here, and it won't take any time to have the tables set up.

"My, I'm glad you've all come! Aren't we going to have a good day?"

"Aside from the schoolgirls, we'll be the youngest ladies here," Alice observed as we looked at the big quilting frame set up in the middle of the room. "We'll get a corner, so we might as well have the one we want."

"Preferably at the end of the quilt that will be tucked under the mattress," said a voice behind us. We turned to find that Augusta Harris had come into the room.

"'I know," she said primly, "everyone has to learn how to quilt sometime in her life. I'm just thankful beginners aren't learning on one of *mine*." She glanced over at me. "And you are . . .?"

"Mabel O'Dell," I replied, and put out my hand. "And this is my friend, Sarah Jane Clark."

Augusta was flustered. "Oh! The new schoolteacher. Well, I wasn't including you, of course. Although I must say you don't look old enough or strong enough to take care of those big boys."

"We're doing nicely, thank you," I said.

Augusta sniffed. "Mm. From what I hear, maybe a little *too* nicely. You'll want to watch your step, young lady." She turned and marched off to join the other women in the kitchen.

"Now what did she mean by that?" I asked in bewilderment.

"Don't pay any attention to Augusta," Alice advised me. "She likes to stir up a little excitement and leave people wondering what she knows. Nine times out of ten she doesn't know anything!"

"I wouldn't be too sure about that this time, Alice."

We turned, and I found myself looking into a pair of cool gray eyes. They belonged to a girl about my age, tall, slender, and very pretty.

"So you are Mabel O'Dell," she said to me. "I must say you're about what I expected you to be." She continued to survey me critically. "I suppose it's that look of innocence that lets you get by with it."

"I don't believe I've met you," I said, feeling my anger rise.

"This is Elizabeth Lawton," Alice quickly interposed.

So this was Elizabeth. I opened my mouth to inquire about what it was I might be getting away with, when Sarah Jane nudged me from behind.

"Don't even ask," she murmured.

Elizabeth swept her cool glance over Sarah Jane and wandered off to talk with someone else.

"My, my," Sarah Jane commented. "You are simply *surrounded* by friends. What have you been doing that I don't know about?"

I was speechless. What had I been doing that even *I* didn't know about?

Alice sighed and led us over to the chairs surrounding the quilting frame. "I had hoped she wouldn't be here today. Her middle name is Trouble."

"Is this the Elizabeth who informed the world that I've set my cap for Len?" I demanded.

Alice looked surprised. "You've heard about that?"

"Not directly," I replied, "but things have a way of getting back to one. What right has she to say something like that? And just where does she get her information?"

"Don't sputter, Mabel," Sarah Jane said. "I don't blame you for being angry, but you can't handle it by getting defensive." Sarah

Jane turned to Alice. "I take it this Elizabeth has her eye on Len for herself?"

Alice nodded. "She has ever since the Lawtons have lived here. Her mother died when Abe was born. Elizabeth was five years old when Cy Lawton married the wife he has now."

Maybe that's the reason for Mr. Lawton's harsh treatment of Abe, I thought. Then I remembered that I was the one being picked on this time.

"Elizabeth has been working and boarding in town since she finished school," Alice continued, "but she's always home on the weekend. She wants to make sure no one else is taking an interest in Len."

"She doesn't need to worry about me," I snapped. "I wouldn't have Len if she gift-wrapped him for me."

Alice looked startled, and Sarah Jane grinned.

"Mabel's upset," she told Alice. "She'll simmer down and start making sense again before long."

I glared at Sarah Jane and jabbed furiously at the quilt in front of me. Even my best friend was against me!

I was forced to pull myself together as more ladies arrived, and I was introduced to the mothers of my students. Mrs. Elliot was a warm, comfortable-looking woman, and I was pleased to tell her how well her boys were doing in school. Prudence and Mrs. Edwards came in, followed by Mrs. Abbot, mother of the twins. I looked around to see if I could locate Mrs. Lawton, but she apparently had not come. The last to arrive was Mrs. Mathews, with Elsie. I liked Amelia Mathews immediately. Her smile was bright, and she grasped my hand eagerly.

"I'm so glad to meet you, Miss O'Dell. Elsie has enjoyed school more this year than she ever has before."

I was surprised, as I hadn't seen much indication that Elsie enjoyed much of anything. What had she been like when she *wasn't* enjoying school, I wondered.

"Thank you," I replied. "Elsie is doing well. She's quieter than most of my students, and that can be a blessing sometimes," I smiled at Elsie and was rewarded with a faint look of pleasure.

They sat down across from us. Prudence came to join Elsie. Soon, everyone was stitching busily and visiting back and forth across the table. I carried on a conversation, but my heart wasn't in it. In spite of myself, my mind kept going back to Elizabeth's remarks. What did I have to feel guilty about?

Sarah Jane's voice broke into my musing.

"Isn't that so, Mabel?"

"Sorry, I didn't hear what you said."

"I know you didn't—that's just what I was telling Alice. You could sit right there, looking alive, and never know if the whole room got up and walked away. Are you still brooding about that Lawton girl?"

"I was not brooding," I replied crossly. "I was thinking. Things are beginning to get out of hand here, and I don't even know why."

"Don't worry about it," Alice advised. "You're doing a good job, and the parents are pleased that you are here. There are always a couple rotten apples in every barrel."

I was comforted somewhat by Alice's words and decided to try to ignore the "rotten apples" and enjoy the rest of the day.

As noon approached, the big tables were set up in the yard, and we began the task of bringing dishes, silverware, and food out from the kitchen. Fried chicken, ham, salads, vegetables, fresh bread, and pies and cakes in abundance were spread across one table. By the time the men and boys began to arrive, the lemonade was ready to pour, and we sat down to enjoy the feast.

Mr. Williams and Len joined us, and I was pleased to note Elizabeth's annoyance that Len had not chosen to sit with her. My pleasure was short-lived, however. As soon as the meal was over, Elizabeth appeared at Len's side.

"Do you have time for a little walk before you go back to work?" she asked him. "I have some plans for next Sunday that I'd like to talk over with you."

"Why, yes, I guess I have time." Len glanced at me, but I looked away and began to talk to Sarah Jane. Elizabeth wasn't going to get a rise out of me. Nevertheless, I felt an unexpected stab of jealousy. I could very easily dislike this girl, and for what reason? After all, I had Russ. Len meant nothing to me.

It was all very confusing, and my heart was not lightened by hearing the voice of Augusta Harris wafting over the table.

"I knew we'd have nothing but trouble with a young lady teaching school. It takes a man to handle a job like that."

I shrugged and looked at Sarah Jane, who squeezed my hand.

"Go get 'em, Mabel," she said, and grinned.

Something
To Think About

OR SEVERAL DAYS THE CHILDREN HAD been playing "pilgrims and Indians" during recess time.

"Did you ever see a pilgrim, Miss O'Dell?" Teddy Sawyer asked me.

"No, but I saw an Indian when I was just a little girl," I replied.

"Did you *really*?" Edward joined in. "What did he look like? Were you scared?"

I told them about the Indian who had visited our cabin and left a beaded basket in exchange for food. Toby Elliot looked apprehensively toward the woods.

"I don't s'pose there's any more left back there."

"No," I assured him, "we aren't likely to have Indian visitors now. And if we did, they'd all be friendly, I'm sure."

"I'd like to see some. I wouldn't be scared." Toby spoke bravely now that there appeared to be no danger from the woods.

"The pilgrims owed their lives to God and the Indians the first year they were here," I said. "That's why they had a Thanksgiving feast and invited their Indian friends."

"And that's why we still have Thanksgiving every year," Hannah put in.

"Don't know why we have to thank God for our crops," Abe Lawton said. "Seems to me we work hard enough to raise 'em."

"You could work twice as hard and have nothing if God didn't send the rain and the sun," I said. "Don't you think God deserves some thanks for the strength we have to work?"

"My pa don't depend on God, and we get the same sun and rain everyone else has," Abe muttered.

"That's true," I agreed. "The Bible says that very thing. God doesn't demand praise from his children, but it pleases him when they remember to give it. Aren't you glad that we have a heavenly Father who loves us even when we forget him?"

The other children nodded solemnly, while Abe stared rebelliously at his desk. My heart ached for him. If his only understanding of a heavenly Father came from his experience with his earthly one, it was small wonder that he felt as he did.

Mr. Clark and Sarah Jane arrived on Wednesday afternoon before Thanksgiving in a flurry of snow. I was packed, ready to go.

"Four whole days at home!" I exclaimed as we drove off. "You can't believe how I've looked forward to this!"

"Oh, yes, I can," Sarah Jane said. "You're not the only one who's going to enjoy having no lessons and no children. I won't even *think* about school until next Sunday afternoon. Will your family all be home tomorrow?"

I nodded. "I'm going to see my nephew for the first time. Reuben is so proud of that boy that he's written twice to tell me how big he's getting. I can't remember Reuben ever writing to me before!"

"Our family will all be home, too. I'll come over after dinner to see the new baby and catch up on the past few weeks." We rode on in silence for a moment; then she continued. "So, how is your friend Elizabeth?"

"Elizabeth who?"

"I'm glad to see you've resolved your differences."

"There are no differences to resolve," I stated. "She goes her way, and I go mine. If that's the kind of girl Len wants, he's welcome to her."

Sarah Jane wisely decided not to pursue that line of conversation, and we talked about other things the rest of the way home.

Russ was due to arrive on Friday after Thanksgiving. I was sure he wouldn't waste much time visiting with Warren's family before he headed for our house.

He appeared at the door shortly after dinner. Ma greeted him warmly and called to me.

"Mabel, Russ is here."

I surveyed myself in the mirror and tucked a stray curl back into place. I was truly glad to see Russ. Why wasn't I more excited?

"Hello, Mabel. It's good to see you," he said stiffly as I entered the room. "You're looking well."

"I am well, thank you," I replied. "Did you have a good trip over?"

"Yes. Yes, very good." He looked nervously around the room. "Say, would you like to go for a walk? It isn't snowing very hard."

"That would be nice," I said. "I'll get my coat."

In my mind I could hear Sarah Jane's mocking voice, "You're certainly off to a galloping start." I smiled. *Not everyone jumps into the middle of things the way you do, my girl,* I answered silently.

Once outside, Russ turned to me eagerly.

"I thought the time would never pass until I could see you," he exclaimed. "I enjoyed your letters, but it's just not the same as being with you. Have you thought about what I mentioned that we need to talk about?"

"Our future?" I nodded. "Yes, I've thought about it."

"Good! Then it's all settled. We'll be married as soon as I finish school!"

I stopped and looked at him in amazement.

"What happened to talking about it?" I asked.

"Oh, we will," he replied happily. "You know I'll be going into the bank with my father when I graduate. He'll build us a house, and you can decorate it any way you'd like. We'll have a good life, Mabel. You'll never lack for anything."

Russ looked so pleased that I hated to burst his bubble.

"I haven't said that I'd marry you, yet," I told him gently. "In fact, I don't believe you even asked me to."

He looked perplexed. "But you knew. What else did you think I had in mind for our future? You do want to marry me, don't you?"

"I don't know, Russ. It's a big decision to make, and I feel I should pray about it. I want to be sure it's the Lord's will for my life."

"*I've* prayed about it, and *I'm* sure," Russ

said, "I never had any idea of marrying anyone else." A thought suddenly occurred to him. "Have you met another fellow? Has he asked for your hand?"

"Of course not, Russ," I laughed. "I'd let you know if I were spoken for. It's just that we still have three and a half years to plan our lives. I think we should be friends now and talk about marriage later. You may find someone in Ann Arbor that you like better, you know."

"Never." He shook his head decisively. "My mind is made up. If I can't have you, I won't have anyone."

"Not even Clarice Owens?" I teased him.

"That doesn't even deserve an answer."

"I'm sorry. That wasn't nice. But you're getting too *serious*, Russ. Come on, let's race to the gate."

We ran down the lane and leaned against the fence to get our breath. The mood was broken, and we spent the rest of the afternoon talking happily about school.

"May I still write to you?" Russ asked as he prepared to leave. "Will you write to me?"

"Certainly. I'm always happy to hear from you. And, Russ, thank you for asking me. I do like you very much, and I'll think about it."

"That's a nice young man," Ma said as we

put supper on the table.

"You need another daughter, Ma. One who could make up her mind before she turned into a spinster."

"I'm not worried about it," Ma replied. "As long as you follow God's timetable for your life, you can't go wrong."

Sarah Jane was philosophical about the matter. "I guess you know what you're doing, Mabel. If Thomas asks me to marry him in three years, I'll say 'yes' immediately, and then think on it. You know about a bird in the hand being worth two in the bush."

"Not if one in the bush looks better than the one in your hand," I retorted. "I do like Russ, and common sense tells me that I could never have a better man in a lot of ways."

"So? What are you waiting for?"

"I don't know," I replied. "I really don't know."

The time between Thanksgiving and Christmas went swiftly. There were so many activities to plan, along with the regular daily work, that I had no time to dwell on my personal problems.

"Miss O'Dell, we have a new girl in school today!" Nancy Lawton met me at the door with the exciting news. "And she's just our size," she added with delight.

I watched as Josie and Rosie escorted a dark-eyed child to the porch. She was poorly dressed, by the standards of the community, wearing only a sweater over her pinafore. Instead of a warm hat, a scarf was over her head, the ends of which were wound around her neck and descended to the hem of her dress. She had no mittens, and her hands were blue with cold.

"Come inside and stand by the stove," I said. "Have you just moved here?"

She nodded.

"What is your name?" I asked as I rubbed her hands.

"Maryanne," she replied softly.

"That's a pretty name." I smiled at her. "That's my mother's name, too. What is your last name?"

"Romani."

Romani. Why did that name sound familiar? I couldn't think why it should nudge something in my memory, so I left Maryanne sitting by the stove and went to call the rest of the children in. When they were all settled with their lessons, I turned my attention to her again.

"Have you been in school before?" I asked.

"No, ma'am."

"Where do you live?"

She pointed vaguely toward the east.

"I think she lives out back of the Abbots' pasture, Miss O'Dell," George Elliot volunteered. "In a wagon."

Teddy snickered, and I glanced at him sharply.

A wagon! My mind went back swiftly to the gypsy family who had stayed on our farm for a week, five years previously. Could this be the same Romani family? The little girl was the right age, and Mrs. Romani could have renamed the baby after Ma when they left. I determined to walk over after school and see. In the meantime, I placed Maryanne with the other beginners, and they were kept busy showing her what they knew.

At dismissal time, Carrie, Elsie, and Prudence wanted me to hear the skit they had prepared for the Christmas program.

"This will use everyone in school, even the beginners," Carrie said. "Do you think it will be all right?"

"It's fine," I told them. "We'll begin practicing tomorrow. With the recitations and songs we have, it should be an excellent program."

"Are you ready to leave, Miss O'Dell?" Elsie asked me.

"Yes, but I'm going to walk over to the Abbots' for a few minutes," I replied. "You go ahead, Elsie. I'll see you in the morning."

112

I locked the big front door and made my way to the Abbots' pasture. Sure enough, there sat the gypsy wagon that Sarah Jane and I had seen that long-ago summer. As I approached, a woman whom I recognized as Mrs. Romani came to meet me.

"Hello, Mrs. Romani. I'm Mabel O'Dell. Do you remember me?"

The look of surprise turned to a bright smile, and she clasped my hand.

"Of course! And you live here now?"

I nodded. "I'm the schoolteacher. When Maryanne came today, I recognized the name. I hoped it might be you."

Mrs. Romani's smile faded. "But where is Maryanne?" she said.

"Why, isn't she here?"

"No, she has not come from school. Did she not leave with you?"

"The smaller children left sometime before I did," I answered. "She must have come home with the twins. Come on, we'll go to the house and get her."

But the Abbot children hadn't seen her. "She didn't come with us. We thought she ran on ahead."

Panic showed in Mrs. Romani's face, and I sought to calm her.

"We'll go back to school. She must be somewhere along the way. There's no place to get off the road between here and there."

The road was empty, and there was no sign of a small girl in a sweater and a shawl. We searched around the school grounds carefully, Mrs. Romani growing more and more frantic as the moments passed.

"Let's look inside," I said as I unlocked the door, "though I'm sure there was no one here when I left."

The room appeared to be empty, but I walked to the front and looked behind my desk. A small sound turned my attention to the big stove in the corner. There lay Maryanne Romani, sleeping soundly on a bench along the wall.

"Here she is," I called, and Mrs. Romani snatched the little girl up and held her closely.

"I thank the Lord that he led me to go and see whether they were the gypsies I knew," I said to Alice and Mrs. Williams later. "That poor child would have been so frightened to awaken in an empty room. She probably would not have come back to school."

"Some people would say it was a coincidence," Alice remarked, "but I believe the Lord directs us. There's nothing too small for his attention."

I agreed, and thought how blessed I was to be able to leave my life in his hands, too.

A Winter
With a Vengeance

WINTER ARRIVED IN EARNEST AFTER the Christmas holidays. It seemed that the snow never stopped falling, sometimes in flurries, sometimes in blizzard-sized flakes. I was thankful for the promised ride to school in the sleigh, for many days the drifts were so deep that walking would not have been possible. The smaller children who had no one to bring them were forced to stay at home.

In spite of what I considered an overabundance, the snow didn't lose its fascination for the children. They bundled up at recess times and found ways to enjoy it. The few times that I was persuaded to join them, I agreed that it was great fun. The boys stamped out a large circle with a cross in the middle to play fox and geese. Before long the track was so slippery that the children were on the ground more than they were running.

Both the boys and girls enjoyed making angels in the new drifts. They would fall back in the snow, and then swing their arms and legs to make wings and a skirt. Help was needed to get up so that the angel was not marred by handprints.

Teddy Sawyer had definite ideas about angels. "I'm not putting any dress on mine," he declared. "Are all the angels in the Bible ladies?"

"I'm sure they aren't," I said. "Gabriel is a man. And the angels who visited Abraham and Sarah were men."

"Who were some of the lady angels?" Julie Ann wanted to know.

"I'm not at all sure about that," I confessed. "I'll have to do some studying about angels. I do know that the Bible says, 'He giveth his angels charge over you, to keep you in all your ways.' That's the most important thing."

"Well, I know I don't want to be one if I have to wear a dress," Teddy muttered. "I'd feel silly, flying around in a skirt."

"You'd look pretty foolish, too," Edward snickered. "Besides, you don't have to worry none about being an angel."

He ducked as Teddy swung at him with both fists, and I quickly stepped in to separate them.

"Why don't you two boys build a big fort and have a snowball fight?" I suggested. "Just remember, no ice balls and no stones in your ammunition."

116

The fort took the rest of the noon recess to construct, and the air was filled with flying missiles whenever the children were outside. All but the most timid entered the fray, and no one suffered more than cold hands and wet feet.

More than winter weather descended with a vengeance during the month of January. The trouble began when Abe arrived at school one morning with his arm in a crudely designed sling.

"Oh, Abe! Did you break your arm?"

He nodded.

"Did you go to a doctor to have it set?"

"No, ma'am. Pa says it'll heal all right without no doctor."

"How did it happen? Did you fall?"

"No, ma'am."

I was determined to find out what had caused his injury.

"Abe, did your father break your arm?" I asked.

Abe hesitated. "Yes'm. But he didn't mean to. He yanked me harder than he thought."

I was appalled. That the man had not only broken his son's arm, but refused to get medical treatment for him, was beyond my understanding. I said nothing more to Abe, but the longer I thought about the situation, the angrier I became. I was still turning it over in my mind as we ate supper that evening.

"Mabel, you aren't eating much tonight. Are you feeling all right?" Mrs. Williams was concerned.

"I feel fine," I replied. "I'm a little upset, is all. Abe came to school today with a broken arm."

"That's too bad," Len said, "but it seems as though most boys break a bone or two before they grow up. Don't worry; it will heal in no time."

"Yes, but this is . . ." I stopped. I couldn't tell these people about Mr. Lawton. If Len was indeed interested in Elizabeth, they wouldn't want to hear it. Or if the information caused Mr. Williams to approach Cy Lawton, I would be in trouble. Maybe it just wasn't my business at all.

"I can see why you're upset," Alice said. "You don't like to see one of your children hurt, even if he is a rough boy."

I looked at her gratefully and nodded. Nothing more was said about the matter, and I tried to take part in the conversation for the rest of the meal. But by the time I was ready for bed, I had decided that this *was* my business, after all. I determined to go and talk to Mrs. Lawton.

118

The next day dragged by slowly, and the fact that another storm appeared to be fathering prompted me to dismiss the children early. In spite of the darkened sky, I turned my steps toward the Lawtons' farm.

I was not prepared for the person who met me at the kitchen door. Mrs. Lawton was a tall, angular woman, hollow cheeked and tired looking. Her clothes were clean, but terribly in need of repair. She carried a baby in her arms, and was followed by a small girl about two years old. She looked both surprised and embarrassed at the sight of me, and I had a momentary feeling of regret that I had not given her warning of my visit.

"You'd be Miss O'Dell, wouldn't you?" she said. "Come in."

I followed her into the crowded kitchen and sat down in the chair she indicated.

"Carrie, you take the baby back and put her to sleep. Julie Ann and Nancy, go play with Ruthie in your room."

When the children had left, Mrs. Lawton turned her attention to me. "I kin see why my husband spends so much time hanging around the school. You're a pretty little thing. Especially compared to what he has at home."

I could feel the blood drain from my face.

"Oh, no! Mr. Lawton doesn't come over to

the school to see me!" I protested.

"What for then?"

"Why, I suppose he comes by to check up on Abe."

Mrs. Lawton shook her head. "He don't care none about Abe."

"Well, I do!" I exploded. "And I think the way his father treats him is nothing short of criminal. How can you stand by and allow it?"

Her face took on a tortured look.

"I can't help it," she said. "Cy says Abe's not my boy, and I'm not responsible for him. He'll raise him the way he sees fit." She looked apprehensively toward the door. "He'll be right angry if he knows you interfered. He'll think we told you. Could we say you come about the girls' schoolwork, if he was to come in?"

"The girls are doing well," I said. "Nancy is reading in the primer, and Julie Ann has improved her arithmetic. You can say I talked about the girls. But I am concerned about Abe, Mrs. Lawton. Isn't there anything I can do?"

She shook her head and motioned me to silence as we heard feet stomping on the porch. The door opened, and a blast of icy wind swept in behind Cy Lawton. He slammed the door shut.

120

"You'll have to do the milking tonight," he said to his wife. "Abe can't do much with one hand." She stood obediently and reached for a heavy sweater and a shawl. Mr. Lawton looked over at me.

"As for you, I guess I know what you're here for. This isn't the time to discuss it. Get your things on and I'll take you home."

I wanted to say, "I'm not your wife, that you can order me around," but I realized that it would not be the better part of wisdom to do so. There was no one here who would keep Cy Lawton from knocking me around as he did his son. Nevertheless, there was no power on earth that would make me accept his offer to take me home.

"I arrived by myself, and I'll go back the same way, thank you."

He eyed me carefully as I wrapped my scarf around my neck and pulled on my heavy mittens. I picked up my books and started for the door. For a moment I thought he was not going to let me out, but then he stepped back.

"Suit yourself, my lady. But don't tell the righteous Williams family that I didn't warn you."

Warn me about what? I thought as Mr. Lawton pulled open the door. Then I stepped out on the porch and saw at once that the storm had turned into a blizzard. The snow felt like ice being driven sideways. There was no visible path ahead of me, and I knew the foolishness of trying to get back to the road over unfamiliar territory. I heard the door close behind me, and considered the possibility of joining Mrs. Lawton in the barn. But the thought of being snowed in with this family and that dreadful man was too much. I had to try to get home, no matter what the odds were against me.

It was completely dark, although I knew it couldn't be five o'clock yet, and by the time I had moved ten paces from the steps, the house was no longer visible. I struck off in the direction I was sure I had come, and after putting the ends of my scarf around my face, I lowered my head and charged into the storm.

I couldn't move very fast. The wind held me back, and the snow drifted in front of me as I watched. Surely there would be some sign of a path made by everyone who had gone in and out today—I had only been in the house twenty minutes! But I could see nothing. I recalled the rope that Pa stretched between the house and the barn during a storm. I had lived long enough in the country to know that one's chances of survival in a blizzard like this were slim indeed.

I had made a mistake: I would swallow my pride—and my fear—and go back to the Lawtons' for shelter. I turned around, but realized with a sinking heart that whatever lay behind me looked exactly like what lay ahead. I had no way of knowing whether I had turned a quarter, a half, or the whole way around. There was no choice but to keep going, regardless of where I was headed.

As I stumbled slowly through the snow, I prayed. "Lord, I'm sorry I was so impetuous. I should have made sure this was the thing you wanted me to do in the first place. I didn't accomplish anything by facing Mrs. Lawton, and now if I die out here in the snow, it will just make things harder for my folks, and the Williamses, and . . . Len. Ma always said my pride would be my downfall, and she was right. Why didn't I tell Len about all this and get his advice? What shall I do now, Lord?"

By this time I had begun to cry, but when I discovered that my tears were freezing on my eyelashes and face, I forced myself to stop. I was cold enough already without producing more ice to carry around.

I had no idea how far I had gone, nor how much time had passed when I sank into snow above my waist. Even when I dropped my books I couldn't scramble out. The harder I tried to climb, the deeper I sank. Breathless, I stopped fighting the snow. *At least,* I thought, *it's warm down here. I've heard of people keeping warm in snow caves. Maybe I'm all right. I'll rest a few minutes, and then try again.*

My next conscious thought was that I ached. My hands, feet, and face were stinging as though I were being pelted with needles. I opened my eyes. Alice and Mrs. Williams were rubbing me briskly. Mr. Williams and Len looked down at me anxiously.

"She's awake. Thank you, Lord," said Mr. Williams.

"Get some warm broth, Alice," Mrs. Williams directed. "We'll have you warmed up in no time, Mabel. You just lie still until the circulation comes back. A good hot bath and a warm bed is what you need."

No one reprimanded me for being out in the storm, nor even asked where I had been. As I sipped the broth, Len told how he had found me.

"I went to school to get you at the regular time, because the storm had already begun," he said. "When I found you weren't there, I remembered how upset you were about Abe. I was pretty sure that's where you had gone. I had the lantern and watched carefully along the road. When I was almost there I saw one of your books, and I figured if the book was there, you were, too. So I got out and dug until I found you. I thank the Lord that I got there in time, Mabel. You weren't far from the Lawtons' home, but they wouldn't have come out looking if they weren't expecting you. They didn't know you were coming, did they?"

I shook my head. "I wasn't going to their house. I was on my way back home."

Len's face grew dark with anger. "You mean you had been at the house, and they let you leave in that storm?"

"I insisted," I said. "I *couldn't* stay there."

"Cy knew you didn't have a chance of getting home by yourself," Len said. "Even someone who's lived here all his life could get lost in that blizzard. He's going to hear about this."

I didn't have the strength to protest, but I knew that my behavior would cause trouble in the community. Perhaps I could think of some way to get things straightened out before the weather cleared.

12

Elizabeth
Causes Trouble

NO ONE WAS SURPRISED WHEN I AWOKE the next morning with a scratchy throat and without a voice.

"There is no place for you to go today, anyway," Mrs. Williams told me as she scurried around fixing a mustard plaster for my chest. "It's still snowing heavily, and the roads are drifted over. You just lie there and rest. You had a horrible experience yesterday."

I was grateful that I didn't have to talk, for I wasn't yet ready to explain about the Lawtons. As I lay in bed and listened to the voices and laughter in the kitchen below, I thought seriously about the situation. What responsibility did I really have? It was obvious that Mrs. Lawton could not—or would not—be of any help. Was it my place to let someone know about the treatment Abe received from his father? What might be the result of such a revelation? Would Cy Lawton have to go to jail, bringing greater hardship on his family?

There seemed to be no answers. I turned restlessly in bed, trying to find a comfortable place for my aching head. My thoughts turned toward home, and how much better I would feel if Ma were taking care of me. Then in my mind I heard Ma's voice, quoting a favorite verse of Scripture: "in every thing by prayer and supplication with thanksgiving let your requests be made known unto God. And the peace of God, which passeth all understanding, shall keep your hearts and minds through Christ Jesus."

"Dear Lord," I prayed, "I do thank you for the times you have answered prayer. I thank you for sending Len to find me last night. You know about the Lawton family and the trouble they have. Help me to leave all that in your hands, and not to worry about it any longer. Thank you, Lord."

I felt a real sense of peace, and soon I drifted off to sleep.

"Mabel?"

I opened my eyes to see Len standing there with a tray in his hands.

"Ma sent you some hot soup. Can you eat a little?"

I did feel hungry, and the aroma wafting across from the bowl was tantalizing. Len put the tray down beside me.

"I'm sure glad the Lord led me to where you were yesterday. You wouldn't have lasted long in that weather. I can't believe those people let you leave the house!"

He shook his head and went back downstairs. As I sipped the warm broth, I decided that I would share what I knew with Len and Mr. Williams as soon as I could talk again. I would not, however, tell him about my encounter with Cy Lawton in the classroom, nor of his frequent appearances around the school yard.

The storm raged for two more days, and it was well toward the end of the next week before the roads were clear enough for us to return to school. I hadn't been home for two weekends, and I looked forward to spending some time with Ma and Pa, and of course, Sarah Jane. I had a lot to tell her.

Since no one had been able to get down to the post office, Len brought home a bundle of mail the day we went back to school. There were three letters from Russ. Although he never mentioned it, I knew that Len was aware how often I heard from Ann Arbor. He also knew that an answer went back each week.

"Mabel, I think you're overlooking a good thing right under your nose," Sarah Jane said when I recounted the events of the past weeks. "Len is a fine person. And he has the advantage of being on the premises."

"Sarah Jane, whose side are you on, anyway? Not long ago you were listing the benefits of being married to a successful banker and having a big house in town. Now you think a penniless preacher is my best choice. Why are you having so much difficulty deciding how to direct my life?"

"You needn't be sarcastic," she replied. "You've always had this problem of halting between two opinions. Goodness knows where you'd be if you hadn't had me all these years. How could you ever run your affairs without my help?"

"It might be interesting to find out," I said, "but of course I never will. As many times as I've told you that I've no intention of marrying *anyone*—least of all a preacher—you insist on making plans in that direction. Whom will you prod into carrying me off— Russ or Len?"

"Don't be ridiculous, Mabel. You know I'd never meddle like that."

I let it pass.

"Anyway," Sarah Jane continued, "you *are* going to tell Len about Cy Lawton, aren't you?"

"Yes, I am. The opportunity hasn't come

yet, but I intend to tell him. None of the Lawtons were in school the two days we were able to get there. They must still have been snowed in."

Everyone was back in place on Monday morning. The weather was bright and beautiful, and I breathed the crisp air with pleasure. Had I known it would be the last undiluted pleasure I would have that day, I might have breathed deeper.

At noon recess, Carrie Lawton approached me.

"Elizabeth says you are to tell Len to come to town and get her tomorrow afternoon."

I was startled. "She *what?*"

Carrie began again patiently. "She says you are to—"

"I heard that," I interrupted. "But why can't *you* deliver the message? Why am I to tell him?"

"Elizabeth said for you to." Carrie shrugged and turned away.

I knew why Elizabeth had sent the communication to me. She wanted to be perfectly sure I knew that Len was her property and that I should keep my hands off. My thoughts churned during the afternoon.

I'll deliver the message to Len, all right, I said to myself as Elsie and I walked toward home after school. But perhaps I could think of some reason I needed to go into town tomorrow afternoon. . . .

"You won't have to worry about Mr. Lawton coming to the school anymore." Elsie's voice broke into my reverie, and I looked at her sharply.

"Whatever do you mean, Elsie?"

"He's gone," she continued complacently. "Carrie says he hasn't been home since right after the storm."

I wanted desperately to know where he was, but I couldn't engage in gossip with a child. I bit my lip and said nothing.

"They don't know where he is," she continued. "Abe says good riddance."

"I'm sure he'll return soon," I said hastily. "There must have been some business to take him away."

"I don't think they'd care if he didn't come back," Elsie replied thoughtfully. "He's not the nicest man to have around, is he?"

I thought that was stating it mildly, but I answered, "We mustn't judge Mr. Lawton or his family, Elsie. We don't know all the facts of the situation."

She nodded in agreement, and we continued on silently.

"Good night, Miss O'Dell," she said when we reached her road. "I'll see you tomorrow."

I walked slowly toward home, my mind in confusion. Should this new development change my resolve to confide in Len? Would it be better to wait until Cy Lawton returned, if indeed he did? It certainly didn't change the problem of Elizabeth, however. I pushed the father to the back of my mind in order to give full attention to the daughter.

While the family was still gathered around the supper table, I entered the conversation with my announcement. "By the way, Len, Elizabeth sent word that she would like you to come to town for her tomorrow afternoon."

They all looked at me as though they had never seen me before.

"Well, I never!" Mrs. Williams exclaimed.

"That sounds like Elizabeth," Alice commented. "Only I can't believe she said she would 'like' you to come. More than likely it was 'you come.'"

I looked down at my plate and smiled to myself at the accuracy of Alice's guess. Len continued to stare at me in disbelief.

"Carrie Lawton brought the message," I told him. "That's all she said."

"I suppose I could do that," Len said slowly. "I don't imagine you'd have a reason to go to town tomorrow, would you?"

My heart flipped over, but I answered demurely, "Why, yes, there are some errands

I could take care of."

The matter wasn't mentioned again that evening, but as I prepared for bed, I was forced to question my motives. Was I pleased because Len seemed to want me with him, or was I delighted to be able to give Elizabeth what I felt she had coming? I had to admit that it was some of each. Whatever the motive, I looked forward to the next day with great pleasure and anticipation.

As I expected, the day crept by like James Whitcomb Riley's reluctant schoolboy. I paid attention to what went on, but my heart wasn't really in it. I was savoring the thought of the surprise Elizabeth had in store.

We left directly after school, and Len kept up a conversation all the way into town. If he felt any irritation at being summoned by a cheeky girl, he gave no indication. Perhaps he really wanted to be at Elizabeth's beck and call, but I couldn't believe that was so.

After we had picked up some things at the general store, Len turned Regal toward the boarding house where Elizabeth stayed. I wasn't disappointed by the expression on her face when she saw me sitting in the sleigh, though I knew it was uncharitable of me to take so much satisfaction in it.

She climbed into the seat with us, and I moved over to give her room. After a cold "Hello," Elizabeth said nothing more till we were back in the center of town. Then she leaned across me and put her hand on Len's arm.

"Oh, Len," she gushed. "Would you mind awfully going into the general store for some white thread? I promised Ma I would bring it, and I forgot to pick it up."

"Why, no, I wouldn't mind," he replied cheerfully. He drew up to the curb and jumped down. Elizabeth kept the smile on her face until he had tied Regal and disappeared into the store. Then she turned to me in a fury.

"Haven't you caused enough trouble?" she hissed.

I had known she would be upset, but this seemed a little out of proportion.

"What have I done?" I asked.

"What have you done? First you get my pa run out of the country. Now you're trying to take Len away from me!"

"I wasn't aware that Len belonged to you," I replied stiffly. "And I don't know anything about why your father left."

"Because of you, of course. You can't be as innocent as you try to act. You led him on, and then had the brass to come right to our house! What else could he do but go away? I'm warning you. You leave Leonard Williams alone, or you'll live to rue the day you came to North Branch!"

Suddenly the smile reappeared on her face. I looked around to see Len emerge from the store carrying the thread.

13

An Unexpected Holiday

ELIZABETH JUMPED DOWN FROM THE sleigh and ran to meet Len. "Oh, thank you!" she exclaimed. "That was so nice of you to do that for me."

Len looked surprised. "It was no trouble at all," he said. "You're welcome."

She followed him around to his side of the sleigh. "You will help me back up, won't you?" she purred. And before I was fully aware of what had happened, I found myself moving over again to make room for Elizabeth in the middle. It was as neat a piece of maneuvering as I had ever witnessed. Len tucked the robe in around us, and we turned toward home.

She chattered lightheartedly the whole way and seemed to have forgotten that I was there, for she never looked in my direction.

The few times in my life before that I had been threatened, I had regarded it as a challenge. This situation was decidedly more complex.

Looking back to my visit with Mrs. Law-

136

ton, I remembered that she, too, had hinted at the fact that I had been responsible for her husband's frequent visits to the school. Now his daughter declared that because of me, he had been forced to leave home! If Elizabeth conveyed this information to Len, what would he think of me? Would I lose my job? The longer I thought about it, the more muddled my mind became, and the further I seemed to be from a solution. By the time the sleigh stopped at the Lawtons' road, and Len got down to walk Elizabeth to the house, my head was aching and I was seriously considering resigning my school and going home to Ma.

Len returned at once, and we proceeded toward home. "You've been awfully quiet," he said to me. "I don't think you said anything all the way back."

"I'm fine. I just have a lot of things on my mind."

Len nodded. "I hope you're not still worried about Abe. You'll likely have more children with broken bones before the year ends."

This was the opening I had waited for to tell Len about Cy Lawton but I found I couldn't do it. Any investigation of the matter would inevitably lead to the information about Mr. Lawton's visits to the school. As far as I knew, Elsie was the only child aware of the situation, and that only because she had walked into the room while he was there, and had observed him lurking about the school grounds. Silently I thanked the Lord that she was not a gabby child.

The following day was cold and crisp.

"Miss O'Dell," the twins announced loudly, "we walked right on top of the fence this morning! And we didn't even go through the snow!" They had arrived, breathless, with Maryanne Romani between them. All three had bright red cheeks and cold noses. No one waited outside on these frigid mornings, but came directly to the stove upon arrival. I helped the girls remove their scarves and boots and settled them with blocks until time for school to begin.

George Elliot carried in more wood for the fire, but in spite of our best efforts the room was bitter cold if one sat more than ten feet from the stove. The older children in the back of the room kept their coats on and blew on their fingers to warm them.

"Look, Miss O'Dell," Nancy said. "Maryanne has gone to sleep."

I glanced over at the little girl, whose desk was nearest the stove. Her head was down on her arms, and she slept peacefully.

"That's all right," I said. "Let her rest. The walk in the cold tired her out. At least she's warm."

When it was time for dinner and Maryanne had not stirred, I went to waken her. As soon as I touched her face, I knew that I should have checked sooner. She was burning hot—much warmer than her nearness to the stove would warrant. I shook her gently, and she opened her eyes.

"Do you want some dinner?" I asked her.

She shook her head. "My throat hurts."

I picked her up and went back to my desk. While I ate, I held her. She put her head on my shoulder and went to sleep again.

"She's breaking out in a rash, Miss O'Dell," Prudence Edwards commented as she stood watching us. "Do you suppose she has the measles?"

"Oh, dear, I hope not. The whole school is likely to get them. She should be at home, though."

"I'll take her," Elsie volunteered. "It isn't very far."

I was grateful, and while I dressed Maryanne for the outdoors, Elsie got ready to go. As an added protection, I wrapped my scarf around Maryanne's head and shoulders. I stood at the door and watched as the girls crossed the school yard and started toward the Romanis' wagon home.

We began the afternoon work reluctantly. If anything, it was colder in the room than it had been in the morning.

"Why is it so cold in here?" Jamie complained. "We need a stove in every corner."

"That wouldn't help," Julie Ann told him. "I'm right by the stove and my feet are frozen. The heat all goes to the ceiling, and we're not up there."

"I know it isn't comfortable," I said. "Finish the lessons you're doing now, and we'll go home early."

I was sure the temperature was dropping, even as we sat here. It would soon be impossible to work. Elsie returned, and a gust of icy wind followed her into the room. The children made a space for her next to the stove.

"I had to carry Maryanne part of the way," she reported. "She never would have made it home by herself. I told Mrs. Romani I thought Maryanne had the measles, but I don't know if she understood me or not."

"Thank you, Elsie," I said. "I appreciate your taking her home. I'll get word to Mrs. Abbot to look in on her later."

I soon decided to send unfinished work home with the children and close the school. When they had all left, I banked the fire, checked the windows, and picked up my books and papers. Elsie had waited, as she usually did, to walk with me.

"Mr. Lawton is back," she said as we started out. "I saw him in the woods when I took Maryanne home."

"Are you sure, Elsie?" I asked her. "Carrie said this morning that he hadn't come home yet."

Elsie nodded. "It was Mr. Lawton, all right."

My heart sank. The children certainly must have been happier while he was gone; at least I was sure that Abe was. My conscience told me that I had no right to make a judgment, but I knew that I was happier when Cy Lawton was not in the vicinity. Perhaps he had come to see how things were at home and would leave again soon.

My black thoughts vanished when I opened the door at home. There at the table with Alice sat Sarah Jane! I dropped my books and hugged her.

"What are you doing here in the middle of the week?"

"The stove at my school has broken down and needs to be repaired," she explained. "No heat, no school. What are *you* doing here in the middle of the afternoon?"

"Same thing," I laughed. "The stove isn't broken, but it wasn't heating the room, either. Oh, it's good to see you! Can you stay the rest of the week?"

Sarah Jane nodded happily, and all of us settled down to visit and enjoy the unexpected holiday. Mrs. Williams lit the lamps against the early darkness, and when Len and Mr. Williams came in shortly before suppertime, I realized I had not once thought about the things that were disturbing me.

"I don't suppose you ladies noticed what's going on outside, did you?" asked Mr. Williams. "I'm glad you closed school, Mabel. There's a sleet storm starting, and unless I miss my guess, we're in for a spell of snappy weather. I think we'll send word that there will be no more school this week."

By Sunday morning the storm was over, and even though the temperature remained below freezing, it was exhilarating to be outside. We arrived at church to find a group of ladies huddled about the stove. Augusta Harris's voice carried easily to the back of the building.

"I warned them that something like this would happen!"

"Now, that's certainly not fair, Augusta!" Mrs. Mathews spoke up. "There was no way she could have known."

"Hmph. Of course not," Augusta replied. "I told them a mere slip of a girl wouldn't have sense enough to run a school."

Sarah Jane poked me. "Sounds like you're the center of attention again, Mabel. What did you do this time?"

The ladies turned and saw us, and Augusta blushed. She was not going to be silenced, though. "Well, I suppose you ladies have heard the news."

"No, Augusta, apparently we haven't. What is it?"

"That little gypsy girl has scarlet fever! And thanks to Miss O'Dell, Elsie Mathews will probably get it, too. Someone with a little common . . . experience wouldn't have let a young girl take care of a child."

Mrs. Mathews came quickly and put her arm around me. "Now don't you pay any mind to Augusta," she said. "There's not one of us would have known that little girl had scarlet fever. You did right to send her home."

I sat down heavily in the nearest seat. Scarlet fever! We had all been exposed. I pictured the children huddled together around the stove, and Maryanne sleeping on my lap. I remembered that Elsie had carried the child part of the way home.

"Oh, I'm sorry," I said. "What can I do?"

"There is nothing to do," Mrs. Williams declared briskly. "This isn't the first time there's been scarlet fever in the community, and it won't be the last. We'll simply ask the Lord to heal and protect."

Len, Alice, and I took Sarah Jane back to her boarding place that afternoon. We talked happily about other things, but underneath lay the dread that there might be an epidemic in the school.

Sarah Jane squeezed my hand as we prepared to leave. "Worrying won't keep it from happening," she said. "I think the Lord wants us to handle things as they come up, not beforehand."

"Sarah Jane, do you feel about ten years older than you did when school started?"

"Oh, at least."

"I'm serious," I said. "I've never had so many problems all at once. I don't get one solved before the next one pops up."

"That's one of the hazards of being on your own," she told me. "We can't get our folks to set things right anymore. We have to depend on the Lord and ourselves.

"Things will turn out just the way they are supposed to, Mabel. Soon you'll be looking back on this year and wondering what the fuss was all about."

14

A Very
Long Week

I WAS RELIEVED TO SEE ELSIE IN SCHOOL ON
Monday morning. The twins were not
there, nor were any of the Lawtons.

"Are the twins ill?" I asked the children.

"No, ma'am," George Elliot told me. "Mrs.
Abbot is afraid that someone else will get
scarlet fever. She wants them to stay home
until the epidemic is over."

"How about the Lawtons?"

No one seemed to know about them. I was
concerned about an epidemic myself, but the
doctor had not advised us to close the school.

"If we were in a spring thaw, I'd say there
might be danger," he said. "This cold weather has slowed it up a bit."

With no wind, the stove kept our room
comfortable, and we worked steadily through
the day. I debated about whether I should
check on the Lawtons after school and decided against it. If Cy Lawton were back, as
Elsie had insisted last week, I certainly
didn't want to run into him. If the children
were sick, I'd hear about it soon enough.

After school, when I had left Elsie at her road, I continued slowly toward home. Len had said he would call to see if the Romanis needed anything, and I was anxious to know how Maryanne was. But I had many things to think through, and walking alone seemed the best opportunity to do it.

A recent letter from Russ had caused me to look back over this year carefully. His plea that we should make plans for our wedding was sounding better and better to me. I had not expected so many conflicts and problems at this small school. Perhaps Sarah Jane had been right about the wisdom of accepting the easy life that Russ was offering. On the other hand . . .

Footsteps sounded behind me, and I turned to find Abe Lawton.

"Abe! You startled me! Where did you come from?"

"I've been following you, Miss O'Dell. I had to talk to you."

"Is something the matter?"

"I'm leaving. I just wanted you to know."

"Why, Abe, where are you going?"

"I don't know. Out west maybe." He shrugged. "Anyplace where my pa ain't."

"Does your mother know?"

"Nope. I'm not telling anyone but you." He looked down at the ground. "You're the only one ever paid any mind to me, 'cept to hit me. Seems like you might like me a little."

"I like you a lot, Abe, and I'll miss you. I understand your wanting to get away. I'll be praying for you. Will you let me hear from you sometime?"

He nodded. "I won't forget you," he said. "I don't think anyone else will miss me." Suddenly, he leaned forward and hugged me. Then he turned and ran into the woods.

My eyes filled with tears as I watched him go. It was ironic, I reflected, that the two students from whom I had expected the most trouble, Abe and Elsie, had turned out to be my staunchest supporters.

As I continued toward the house, I decided to say nothing about seeing Abe. I was sure no one would inquire about him, or be surprised when they found he had left home again.

At suppertime, Len reported that he had been to see the Romanis.

"Where they put themselves and three children in that wagon, I'll never know. I didn't go inside, but Mrs. Romani stepped out to talk to me. Through the door I could see that Maryanne is pretty sick. The doctor comes by each day. He's sure the boys will have the fever in a week or so."

"I don't see how they could help it, staying

in cramped quarters like that," Mrs. Williams remarked. "I wish they had a house to live in. Do they need food or blankets or anything we can take to them?"

Len shook his head. "She says not. But she seemed pleased that I had come."

School went on as usual. No one else became ill, and it seemed that there would be no epidemic after all. The Lawtons returned, and aside from the announcement by Julie Ann that Abe had run away again, nothing more was said about his absence. I wondered if the girls were not relieved that Abe was no longer there to be knocked around by his father.

By this time I should have been ready for anything that could happen, but I was totally unprepared on Friday when I looked up and saw Elizabeth Lawton standing in the door. It was noon recess, and the children were scattered about the school yard, enjoying the sunlight and cold air. She walked up to the desk, regarding me coldly.

"You don't pay much attention to what people say to you, do you? I thought I warned you about staying away from my family."

I looked at her blankly. She *could* surprise me again. Since I had no idea what she was talking about now, I didn't say a word.

"Did you think no one would see you, right out on the road, hugging my brother? Just who do you think you are? Isn't it enough that you're openly chasing Len?"

Suddenly I felt that I had taken about as much from her as I needed.

"I think it's time that you understood something," I told her. "I have no designs on your father *or* your brother, and you know that as well as I do. And as for Leonard Williams, when he decides to find a girl to marry, it will be *his* choice, not ours. If you can't stand the thought of his having more than one friend, that is your problem, not mine. Now I'd appreciate it if you'd find someone else to threaten. I'm tired of it."

She looked at me with astonishment.

"Well. You do have a little spunk, don't you? But if you think you've heard the last from me, you're mistaken. I want Len, and I mean to have him."

She whirled around and left the room. I was more shaken by the encounter than I let her know, but I wasn't sorry I had spoken my mind. I really didn't think that Len had any interest in me—but Elizabeth Lawton would never find that out if I could help it.

I was happy to go home for the first time in three weeks. Mr. Clark and Sarah Jane were waiting for me when I came in from school.

Sarah Jane surveyed me critically. "You look like the breaking up of a hard winter, Mabel," she said. "Do you feel as bad as you look?"

"I'm fine," I snapped. "All I need is a few days in a calm, quiet atmosphere with no problems, no decisions, no accusations, no questions . . ."

"In other words, you're ready to depart for heaven immediately." Sarah Jane laughed. "I don't think you look quite *that* bad. Come on, get your things together and we'll take you home to your mother. She'll straighten you out."

"I'm sorry, Sarah Jane," I said. "I shouldn't jump on you, but this has been one *horrid* day. It's almost as though I have to pay for the good time we had last week. I'll be all right once we get started toward home."

Sarah Jane was delighted when I told her of my conversation with Elizabeth. "Good for you, Mabel!" she said. "It's time you stood up and made yourself heard."

"You know I hate conflict," I said glumly, "but I can't stand by and have my character maligned. Why does she persist in thinking that I'm out to get Len?"

"Well, Mabel, maybe she sees that he's interested in you."

150

"Don't be ridiculous, Sarah Jane! Len has never indicated in any way that he wants to be more than a friend."

"You won't see what you won't see," she said with a sigh. "After all these years, I would think you'd begin to trust me. And I say you care more about Len than you're letting yourself admit."

There was no future in arguing with her. The disconcerting truth remained that she usually *was* right.

Ma was happy to see me. "I still haven't gotten used to this big house with just Pa and me in it," she said. "I see the boys every day, but it's not the same." She looked reflectively around the kitchen. "It's been a long time since I've mopped the floor twice in one day."

"I can't believe you miss that," I laughed. "You have time to do things for yourself now. Don't you enjoy it?"

"Of course," she replied, "I'm not complaining. I just meant that it was . . . different."

I can't wait for summer to come, I thought. Ma and I could both stand a few weeks of having things the way they used to be.

Sunday afternoon came too quickly, and Pa took us back to school. "This week will be better, Mabel," Sarah Jane assured me as we left her at Edenville. "At least, it certainly couldn't be worse."

For once, Sarah Jane was wrong.

Mrs. Williams appeared on the porch before I could get out of the sleigh.

"I'm sorry, Mabel," she said, "but you can't come in. Leonard has scarlet fever."

"Oh, no!" I gasped. "When . . . ?"

"He came down with it Saturday. Fortunately Alice was gone for the weekend, too. Augusta Harris has offered to let you girls stay with her until the quarantine is lifted."

"Why is everything falling in on me at once?" I asked Pa as we rode on toward Augusta's house. "Is the Lord sending all this to tell me something?"

"I know it must seem like that to you," Pa replied, "but I don't think the Lord works that way. If he's trying to tell you anything, I'd say it would be that his grace is sufficient. That's not a bad message."

"I'll need all the grace I can get, living in the same house with Augusta," I said. "Come to think of it, she will, too. She thinks I'm an irresponsible knobhead who has no business being in charge of a school. I'm certainly glad Alice will be there with me."

I didn't say so to Pa, but I was terribly worried about Len. I realized how much I looked forward to seeing him every evening and how I enjoyed talking to him. The memory of his discreet silence about how we had met and his laughing eyes when something reminded us of that time came flooding back.

Pa's promise to pray for me and for the Williams family comforted me as I moved my things into Augusta's spare room.

"You girls will have to make do with what I have," she informed us. "It may not be all you're used to, but beggars can't be choosers."

"I'm sure it will be just fine, Augusta," Alice said. "We appreciate your taking us in. I'm sure it was the Lord's timing that we weren't in the house when Len got sick. We'll try to stay out of your way."

You can count on that, I added silently. I was sure Augusta would find something to complain about, but I didn't plan to deliberately provoke her.

I woke Monday morning with a heavy feeling, and then remembered where I was and why. I prayed for special strength to get through the day at school. Alice and I planned to walk home every afternoon to see how Len was. Since Mr. Williams couldn't leave the farm, we would pick up the mail and run errands.

To my surprise, Augusta was kind to us. The little barbed remarks continued, but she seemed eager to help. During the day she sewed with Alice; in the evening she graded papers for me. She was as distraught as we were over Len's condition, for he seemed to be getting worse every day.

It took all the courage I could summon to get through each school day. My prayers alternated between pleas for Len's recovery and thankfulness that none of the other children had gotten scarlet fever. It was a very long week indeed.

15

Mrs. Lawton
Speaks Out

L AND SAKES, MABEL! IF YOU AREN'T EX-
hausted, I am. Can't you sit down for
ten minutes at least?" Augusta stirred
the stew that bubbled on the stove as she
watched me make my hundredth trip to the
window.

"I can't help it, Augusta. Dr. Mason went
over there last night. He promised he'd stop
on the way back and tell us how Len is. Why
hasn't he come?"

"Wearing out my kitchen floor won't bring
him any faster," she said. "You're not going
to be fit to go to school tomorrow if you don't
settle. I know you're worried," she added a
little more kindly, "but Len is in the Lord's
hands. There's nothing any of us can do but
trust."

"I know," I replied. "Sarah Jane always
reminds me that patience is not my most
prominent virtue. But whatever will I do if
Len should die?" Suddenly I burst into a
flood of tears, and Augusta turned back to
the stove, embarrassed.

Alice hurried to put her arm around my shoulder. "Len is young and strong," she said. "Many people have lived through scarlet fever. And remember that the Lord says, 'My strength is made perfect in weakness.' You know he'll never send us more than we can bear, with his help."

"That's right," Augusta chimed in. "Don't borrow trouble. When Len dies, *then* you worry about what you'll do."

Alice glared at Augusta, but I had to smile at her attempt to encourage me. "You're right, Augusta. I should have more faith." I wiped away my tears. "I'll set the table for supper. That will redeem the time, won't it?"

Augusta nodded. "And while you're at it, set a place for the doctor."

I busied myself with the dishes and silverware. While I was slicing the bread, Alice called from the window.

"He's coming, Mabel."

I rushed for the door and, ignoring the freezing cold, raced out into the yard to meet the doctor as he descended from the sleigh.

"Is he all right? Is Len all right?"

"Do you want to get sick, too? We can't stand out here in the cold and talk." Dr. Mason hurried me back into the kitchen, and when he had taken off his heavy coat, he sank heavily into a chair.

"Len is going to get well," he said, and I dissolved into tears again.

This time Augusta looked disgusted. "If you don't beat all. Ten minutes ago you were wailing because you thought Len would die; now you're blubbering because he didn't." She shook her head. "I'm certainly glad I was never a foolish young girl."

"Your memory is short, Augusta," the doctor commented.

Augusta sniffed, and as she went back to the stove, I saw her wipe her cheek with the edge of her apron.

The doctor turned back to us. "I was afraid we were going to lose him last night. He's had a terribly high fever, but it dropped toward morning and he's resting now. It will take awhile for him to regain his strength, but he's on his way. I think you girls can go back home in another week."

Supper was a joyous meal. Len was getting better! I couldn't wait to get back home.

When we packed our things to leave, Augusta was sorry to see us go, although she didn't admit it in so many words.

"There are advantages to living alone," she said. "When you find a hair in the honey, you know it's your own. But I recognize my duty when I see it. If you need shelter again, I can make room for you. I imagine it will seem pretty quiet for a while, without all your chatter. Not that I couldn't stand a little peaceful silence."

Impulsively I hugged her. "You've taken good care of us, Augusta. We really appreciate it. We'll miss you."

"Oh, pshaw. I only did what any decent Christian would do. Of course, I know some very good Christians who couldn't live with two flibbertigibbets for three weeks."

The Williamses were glad to welcome us home.

"These have been the longest three weeks of my life," Len's mother admitted. "I couldn't have gotten through it if I hadn't known that everyone was praying for us. But now spring will soon be here, and everything will be back to normal."

I was shocked at how white and thin Len looked, but he smiled brightly.

"Aren't you glad I was so considerate as to get sick while you were both gone?" he asked. "I usually like to share whatever I have with my loved ones, but I was glad to make an exception this time."

I couldn't find an answer to his comment. Did his "loved ones" include me? Or was that just a chance phrase?

With the coming of spring, Russ's letters

became more frequent and more insistent. I shared the latest letter and my uncertainty with Sarah Jane.

Dear Mabel,

We will be having a week's holiday in April, and I would like to spend some time with you. I thought you'd want to know that my father has purchased land for our house. As soon as we decide on the plans, the building can begin. I know you wanted more time before we set a date, but you can see how important it is to start planning for the future. The next three years will go by so quickly.

"You seem to be the only one who hasn't made up her mind," Sarah Jane commented. "Russ and his father certainly have no doubts."

"I know," I replied, "and common sense tells me that I should be enthusiastic about his offer. After this year, I'd enjoy having someone look after me. I *like* Russ. I could live with him and be happy. What am I waiting for?"

"I think you're waiting for someone you can't live *without*," Sarah Jane said. "Or maybe you've already found him."

"Len?" I shook my head. "I may feel that

way, but he doesn't. I didn't realize how much I thought of him until I was afraid he might die. Besides, the first time I saw him—no, it was the second time—he said he would never ask anyone to share what he makes as a country preacher."

"I seem to recall your saying you'd never marry a minister, either," Sarah Jane reminded me. "*Never* must be the most often-eaten word in the English language. I guess you have to decide whether you'll settle for a sure thing and accept Russ, or hold out for what you really want, and wait for Len."

"You're a bundle of help. If you had to make a choice between Thomas and someone else, you wouldn't think it was such an easy decision."

"True. But it would be *my* choice. I can't make up your mind for you, Mabel."

"I don't believe what I hear," I told her. "Since when are you reluctant to set me on the right way?"

Sarah Jane looked serious. "This is a matter of your entire future life," she replied. "I can't be responsible for that."

Though I had not seen him, Cy Lawton was indeed back home. When I walked to school one morning several weeks later, I found him standing by the school-yard fence.

160

He opened the gate and followed me into the yard. I was not about to be followed into the building, so I waited by the steps to see what he wanted.

"I don't suppose you know where Abe went."

"No, I don't."

"And I don't suppose you'd tell me if you did," he continued.

"Why would you want to know?" I burst out indignantly. "Apparently the boy was nothing but an irritation to you. You should have been reported for the way you treated him."

"I was reported," Cy replied. "Elizabeth thinks it was you as done it."

"Elizabeth is wrong. I've not talked to anyone but your wife. If I were going to tell someone, I wouldn't have waited until Abe was gone to do it."

Cy regarded me silently. "You're pretty little to be so sassy," he said finally. "I just come by to tell you that if Abe shows up, and there's a trial, you'd better keep your mouth shut. How I bring up my boy ain't none of your business, and if I was you, I wouldn't meddle. You understand?"

I was frightened, but the anger I felt overshadowed the fear. "Good day, Mr. Lawton," I said. "I have work to do."

I was thankful to see some of the children approaching, and to watch Cy Lawton disappear in the opposite direction. When I reached my desk, I was trembling so that I couldn't put the day's lessons on the board for several minutes. I had decided that since Abe was gone, I would not need to say anything to Len or Mr. Williams about what I knew. Now I was not so sure. As far as I was aware, Abe was the only member of the family who had actually been mistreated. But Cy Lawton was dangerous. It might no longer be safe to keep the matter to myself.

When I returned home in the afternoon, I found Mrs. Lawton seated in the kitchen with Len and his parents.

"I'm glad you're home, Mabel," Mr. Williams said. "This concerns you, too. Mrs. Lawton has told us why you were visiting her the day of the storm. You did the right thing by trying to have the problem settled inside the family, but you should have let us know that Cy was coming to the school. You could have been in danger."

"She says that Cy thinks you reported him to the authorities," Len put in. "She was afraid he would try to see you about it."

I sat down at the table. "He did," I said. "He was there this morning." I repeated the conversation between us, and told Len and

Mr. Williams all I had observed until the time Abe left. I did not mention the main reason for my silence—that I was afraid that Len might really care about Elizabeth.

Mrs. Lawton listened to my story, and then she spoke. "Elizabeth doesn't know," she said, "but I'm the one who reported Cy. When he turned Miss O'Dell out into the storm, I couldn't stand it no more. He left home because he thought he'd be held responsible if she died. She didn't, so he came back. That's when I made up my mind to speak out."

Mr. Williams looked grim. "I thank you, Mrs. Lawton, for coming here. I'll see that this matter is taken care of."

The relief I felt was overwhelming. I had been more frightened than I would honestly admit, even to myself.

16

The Choice
Is Made

APRIL WAS A MONTH OF MANY MOODS. Bright sunlight, sudden showers, and mud. In spite of Mr. Elliot's best efforts, our room looked like a back pasture. I finally concluded that it would be better to overlook the muddy boots and shoes that tracked in and out all day. When it dried, the dirt was swept outside and the cycle began again. I did, however, insist that hands be washed before the children came to class.

"My pa says you'll eat a pound of dirt before you die," Jamie informed us.

"You don't have to have it all at once," I said. "Try to spread it out over your lifetime. Besides, we need to keep our books looking neat. They have to last a long time."

While the children were busy with their lessons, I gazed out the window at the early spring day. the annual program for the school board and parents was to be given the third Friday of this month—just two weeks away.

I wasn't worried about the children doing

164

well; I knew they were prepared and anxious to please. I felt that I had been conscientious and successful in my first year.

Carrie Lawton approached me at the beginning of the week. "My pa says he ain't coming to the program," she said.

"I'm sorry to hear that," I replied. "You, Julie Ann, and Nancy have done fine work this year. Will your mother be able to come?"

Carrie shook her head. "Pa won't let her. He says we wouldn't be here, either, if the law didn't make us."

I was sure that was true. It would be a miracle if any of the girls in that family ever went to high school.

"But Elizabeth is coming. She says Leonard Williams is going to bring her." Carrie searched my face for my reaction.

I forced myself to smile. "I'm sure we'll have a nice group of people here to enjoy the program. I'm counting on you to win the spelling bee for the school."

Elizabeth again. I didn't know why I had assumed that Len would be coming with me that evening; It hadn't been mentioned between us. It occurred to me that perhaps Len did not even know he was bringing Elizabeth, but I dismissed the thought. She wouldn't say so if he hadn't asked her.

At home, Alice was in a flurry of activity. Her wedding was to be in May, and Augusta was coming in daily to help with the sewing.

"We'll be doing this for you next," Augusta said to me, "though I can't see why you girls want to rush into things. You'll have your whole life to be tied down to a house."

"If I weren't tied down to a house, I'd be tied down to a school, Augusta," Alice laughed. "And I wouldn't call two years rushing into things."

"I suppose not," Augusta conceded. "You're pretty levelheaded." She looked over her glasses at me. "Have you made up your mind about your young man?"

"I'm happy being tied down to a school, Augusta. Why should I look for something else?"

"That's a fine speech," she replied. "I don't believe a word of it."

Neither did Sarah Jane. "You should let Len know how you feel about him, Mabel. He's not going to speak out if he thinks you don't care."

"Sarah Jane," I said with a sigh. "How long have we been friends?"

"About nineteen years."

"Would you like it to continue for another nineteen? Because if you would, don't make

166

silly suggestions like that. You *know* I'm not going to throw myself at Len."

Sarah Jane whooped with laughter. "I'm glad you said that instead of me!"

"Don't you dare say what you're thinking," I warned her. "That is in the forgotten past."

"Past maybe, but certainly not forgotten," she gasped. "Come on, Mabel, you have to see the funny side of it. Very few people are privileged to meet the love of their life under such auspicious conditions."

"Very few people have someone to take care of all the details of their future, either," I replied. "How could I be so lucky?"

The evening of the program arrived before I was ready for it. Nothing had been said about Len taking Elizabeth. While he was busy getting dressed, I hurried over to the school. It wouldn't hurt to be there early and be sure that all was ready.

Families soon began to arrive, and I was kept occupied greeting them and trying to calm the excited children. I wasn't aware that Len had arrived until he appeared at my side.

"You left before I knew it, Mabel," he said. "I intended to walk over with you. I thought you might need some help getting ready."

I looked up to see Elizabeth hovering in

the background. "Thank you," I said airily. "I got along just fine. Everything is under control."

Len looked disappointed, but he went to sit down. Elizabeth sat down beside him.

I'll just keep my eyes on the children and not pay any attention to them, I thought. *It's none of my affair that he chose to come with her.*

The room was soon filled, and Mr. Williams, as school board president, opened the program with prayer. It was time to begin the evening's entertainment.

As I rose to lead the beginners to the front for their part, the door opened, and Russ Bradley stepped into the room. My heart flopped, and I could feel my face getting warm. What was he doing here? He had said he would call at home on Sunday.

The children did well, though I probably wouldn't have noticed if someone had made a mistake. My mind was in such a whirl that the congratulations of the parents hardly registered. It seemed like hours before the schoolroom cleared out, and I was left alone with Russ.

He took both of my hands in his. "I know you weren't expecting me tonight, Mabel, but I couldn't wait until Sunday to see you. Warren loaned me a buggy, so I thought I could take you home in the morning. May I?"

He looked so hopeful that I hadn't the heart to tell him no. Some time ago Len had offered to drive me home, and I had been looking forward to it. Of course, he might have just been doing the polite thing. For all I knew, he might have asked Elizabeth to accompany us!

"Of course you may," I said to Russ. "It was nice of you to come."

"We have a lot to talk about," Russ went on. "I hope you're ready to consider announcing our engagement."

Why not? I thought wearily. He was so positive; it seemed more effort than it was worth to find reasons why I should wait longer. I opened my mouth to say yes, when he stopped me.

"Don't answer now, Mabel. I want to talk to your father first. We'll leave early in the morning, shall we?" He looked around the empty room. "You certainly won't be missing this. I'd think one year of teaching would be enough. I'd rather you stayed home until we were married. Are you ready to go now?"

I nodded, and we went out into the night. We would talk later. Things were not going as I wanted them to, but I felt powerless to do anything about it. And I was too tired to think any farther ahead than the moment.

Russ left me at the door and went into town to spend the night. A lamp was burning on the table, and I picked it up to light the way to my room.

"Mabel?"

Len's voice stopped me at the stairway. "I've been waiting for you to come home. Could we talk before you go to bed? If you're not too tired, that is."

Suddenly I was not at all tired. I came back to the table, and we sat down facing each other. Len was ill at ease, but he cleared his throat and spoke.

"I wasn't prepared to say anything like this," he began, "but when I saw the way that fellow Russ looked at you tonight, I knew I had to. Mabel, I haven't anything to offer you but just myself. You know I'm called of the Lord to do his work, and the payment in this life is exceedingly small. There would be no big house or money to spend on luxuries. I'm selfish even to ask you to share a future as bleak as that.

"But since the first time I saw you, I knew you were the only one for me. I've wanted to tell you so many times this year, but I didn't dare, knowing that you were spoken for."

He brushed his hair back nervously. "I shouldn't be saying this now, but somehow I felt that this was the time. Mabel, would you consider marrying me in a year or so?"

"Oh, Len," I replied. "There's no one I'd rather have. I didn't know how I'd live without you once you married Elizabeth."

"Elizabeth!" Len exclaimed. "Whatever gave you the idea that I would marry her?"

"She did, I guess. You hadn't said that you *weren't* courting her."

"I didn't realize I needed to. I never dreamed you'd think I was interested in anyone except you."

"It doesn't matter now," I said. "We both know that the Lord has brought us together. He was the one who made sure you spoke tonight, Len. I was ready to tell Russ tomorrow that I would accept his offer."

We talked for a long while before I made my way upstairs. I couldn't remember ever having been happier. Len promised to come on Sunday to bring me back, after agreeing that I must go home with Russ as planned.

"I don't understand," Russ said, when I told him as gently as possible that I couldn't marry him. "If you've been planning on someone else all along, why didn't you tell me?"

"But I haven't been, Russ. I've prayed and considered your offer very carefully. I know you would have done all you could to make me happy, but I've never been as *sure* of anything as I am now about this."

He nodded dismally. "I understand. I'm not happy, but I understand. I wish you all the best in your life."

"Thank you, Russ. You have three more years before you're free to marry, and I know the Lord has the right person for you, too."

He looked unconvinced, but when we parted at my porch, he shook my hand warmly. "I'll not forget these years, Mabel. You've been a wonderful friend."

"I won't forget them, either," I told him. "It's part of both our lives that nothing will ever change."

My nineteenth birthday dinner was over, and Sarah Jane and I were sitting under our favorite tree. "A year ago today you declared that you wouldn't consider marriage for years and years, if ever," she mused. "And now suddenly, here you are, the first one to marry. You planned it all along, didn't you?"

"You know better than that," I laughed. "Besides, we'll not be getting married for two years at least. You and Thomas will have your wedding as soon as he's out of school. Isn't everything turning out the way you wanted it to?"

"Well . . . I was looking forward to visiting

you in that big house in town. But I suppose if you must consider *whom* you live with rather than where you live . . ."

I looked at her fondly. "Sarah Jane, you are impossible. What would I ever do without you?"

"My thoughts exactly," she nodded. "Now let me tell you what to do next. . . ."

She grinned and covered her head with her arms as I pounced on her.

Away from Home

Away from Home

When you're sixteen, everything is momentous.

That's what Mabel's best friend Sarah Jane tells her as they begin their first year of school at the academy in town. Away from their farm homes and families for the first time, the two girls must contend with a new school, new acquaintances, and new ways of doing things.

And Sarah Jane is right. Whether it's wearing bloomers for physical culture class, mustering the courage to invite young men to an evening social event, or helping the housekeeper with a routine task, the two friends have a way of making "momentous moments" out of anything. Mabel and Sarah Jane rise to each occasion with their usual measure of hilarity, anguish, and newfound insights, all the while learning more of what it means to place one's trust in God.

The Grandma's Attic Novels bring you the story of Mabel O'Dell's young adult years as she becomes a teacher, wife, and mother. Be sure to read all five!

Away from Home
A School of Her Own
Wedding Bells Ahead
At Home in North Branch
New Faces, New Friends

Gifted storyteller **Arleta Richardson** grew up an only child in Chicago, living in a hotel on the shores of Lake Michigan. Under the care of her maternal grandmother, she listened for hours as her grandmother told stories from her own childhood. With unusual recall, Arleta began to write these stories for an audience that now numbers over 2 million. "My grandmother would be amazed to know her stories have gone around the world," Arleta says.

Cook Communications

GRANDMA'S
ATTIC NOVELS
◆

Wedding
Bells Ahead

Wedding Bells Ahead

Just a few more months as Miss O'Dell . . .

Mabel is engaged to Len Williams and looks forward to a peaceful second year of teaching. But in order to keep the school she loves, she needs a place to live. Her only choice seems to be boarding with Augusta Harris, whose favorite pastime is keeping track of everyone else's business.

A big storm, a buried will, old rumors, and new schemes contrive to make Mabel's year anything but dull. And suddenly Len faces an unexpected decision—one that will affect both of their lives.

Through it all, Mabel's best friend Sarah Jane is still nearby, ready to offer a fresh perspective and a reminder that God is in control of every detail.

The Grandma's Attic Novels bring you the story of Mabel O'Dell's young adult years as she becomes a teacher, wife, and mother. Be sure to read all five!

Away from Home
A School of Her Own
Wedding Bells Ahead
At Home in North Branch
New Faces, New Friends

Gifted storyteller **Arleta Richardson** grew up an only child in Chicago, living in a hotel on the shores of Lake Michigan. Under the care of her maternal grandmother, she listened for hours as her grandmother told stories from her own childhood. With unusual recall, Arleta began to write these stories for an audience that now numbers over 2 million. "My grandmother would be amazed to know her stories have gone around the world," Arleta says.

Cook Communications

At Home in North Branch

At Home in North Branch

At home in North Branch—what could be better?

Happy with Len in their little house by the river, surrounded by friends, Mabel is content with her life as a schoolteacher and minister's wife in the small logging community. But a storm is about to break over North Branch, and no one in town will be left untouched.

Meet Rowland Brewer, the new manager of the shingle mill: handsome, friendly . . . and just a shade too smooth. Meet his daughter, Daisy: the sweetest, prettiest ten year old ever seen . . . at least at first glance.

And get reacquainted with the Lawton clan, still holding a grudge against Mabel . . . Augusta Harris, still keeping track of everyone's comings and goings . . . and of course Sarah Jane, who has moved back into Mabel's life to remind her that the Lord will help her weather every trial.

The Grandma's Attic Novels bring you the story of Mabel O'Dell's young adult years as she becomes a teacher, wife, and mother. Be sure to read all five!

Away from Home
A School of Her Own
Wedding Bells Ahead
At Home in North Branch
New Faces, New Friends

Gifted storyteller **Arleta Richardson** grew up an only child in Chicago, living in a hotel on the shores of Lake Michigan. Under the care of her maternal grandmother, she listened for hours as her grandmother told stories from her own childhood. With unusual recall, Arleta began to write these stories for an audience that now numbers over 2 million. "My grandmother would be amazed to know her stories have gone around the world," Arleta says.

Cook Communications

GRANDMA'S
ATTIC NOVELS

New Faces,
New Friends

New Faces, New Friends

Who says a small town is a dull place to live?

The logging community of North Branch, Michigan, is still a small town in 1895. But Mabel and Len Williams and their circle of friends could never be called bored. . . .

Mabel finds that her position as the minister's wife doesn't protect her from small town gossip. After all, isn't it a little odd that Hudson Curtis, pastor of a neighboring church, happens to show up every time Mabel comes to town? And wasn't that his buggy seen turning down Mabel's lane the other afternoon? Even Mabel's best friend, Sarah Jane, seems troubled about something—but for the first time in her life, she won't discuss it with Mabel.

Good thing Mabel knows she can trust God in the troubled times as well as the good.

The Grandma's Attic Novels bring you the story of Mabel O'Dell's young adult years as she becomes a teacher, wife, and mother. Be sure to read all five!

Away from Home
A School of Her Own
Wedding Bells Ahead
At Home in North Branch
New Faces, New Friends

Gifted storyteller **Arleta Richardson** grew up an only child in Chicago, living in a hotel on the shores of Lake Michigan. Under the care of her maternal grandmother, she listened for hours as her grandmother told stories from her own childhood. With unusual recall, Arleta began to write these stories for an audience that now numbers over 2 million. "My grandmother would be amazed to know her stories have gone around the world," Arleta says.

Cook Communications